the YGGYSSEY

How Iggy Wondered What Happened to All the Ghosts, Found out Where They Went, and Went There

by DANIEL PINKWATER

Illustrations by

Calef Brown

sandpiper

HOUGHTON MIFFLIN HARCOURT
Boston   New York

www.hmhbooks.com

The text of this book is set in Apollo.
The illustrations were created in brush and ink.

The Library of Congress has cataloged the hardcover edition as follows:
Pinkwater, Daniel Manus, 1941–
The Yggyssey / by Daniel Pinkwater ; [illustrations by Calef Brown].
p. cm.
Summary: In the mid-1950s, Yggdrasil Birnbaum and her friends,
Seamus and Neddie, journey to Old New Hackensack, which is on another
plane, to try to learn why ghosts are disappearing from the Birnbaum's
hotel and other Hollywood, California, locations.
[1. Adventure and adventurers—Fiction. 2. Ghosts—Fiction. 3. Witches—
Fiction. 4. Space and time—Fiction. 5. Haunted places—Fiction. 6. Hotels, motels,
etc.—Fiction. 7. Hollywood (Los Angeles, Calif.)—History—20th century—
Fiction.] I. Brown, Calef, ill. II. Title.
PZ7.P6335Ygg 2008
[Fic]—dc22
2008001874

ISBN 978-0-618-59445-0
ISBN 978-0-547-32865-2 pb

Manufactured in the United States of America
EB 10 9 8 7 6 5 4 3 2 1
4500213674

CONTENTS

CHAPTER 1

Room Full of Spooks

When I got home from school, my room was full of ghosts
. . . again! They were being invisible, but I could feel the
cold spots in the air.

"Did I speak to you ectoplasms about this, or did
I not?" I asked the empty room.

Silence. The ghosts were dummying up.

"Rudolph Valentino! I can smell your lousy
cigar!"

There was a faint smell of cigar smoke, the trademark
of the ghostly Valentino, so I knew he was among them.
And my bedspread was rumpled. Probably they were sitting on my bed, playing cards.

"Look, you spectres—this is a young girl's bedroom,

not a club! Why do you have to hang out here all the time? You have an eight-story hotel to haunt. There's a complete apartment reserved for your personal use. Why don't you stay there? It's the nicest one in the whole building." The management had sealed off a large apartment because it was way too haunted for living guests to put up with. The hope was that if they gave the ghosts their own space they wouldn't haunt the rest of the hotel so much. Some hope.

"We get bored," Rudolph Valentino said. "It's nothing but ghosts there."

"So you crowd in here so you can bore me, and stink up my room," I said. I was mad. I really liked most of the ghosts, but a woman is entitled to some privacy. Grumbling and mumbling, the ghosts climbed out my bedroom window, made their way along the ledge, and climbed into the window of the apartment that had belonged to Valentino in 1927. I had been in the apartment lots of times. Like the ghosts, I had to climb out my window and go along the narrow ledge to get in, which was a little scary to do if you weren't already dead.

The Hermione is not a regular hotel in the sense that people check in for a couple of nights or a week. It's all apartments, some tiny and some quite large. People live in it for months at a stretch, or all the time. It was quite the fancy address when my father first came to Hollywood in the days of the silent movies.

You can see what a deluxe sort of place it was. It has

architecture all over it. There are rough plaster walls, old-fashioned light fixtures made of hammered iron, fancy tile floors, and dark, heavy woodwork with carvings and decorations on it. There are tapestries that hang from iron things that look like spears, and a couple of suits of armor standing around. It looks like a movie set. It's a combination of old Spanish California and the Middle Ages, with some *Arabian Nights* thrown in.

I have lived in the Hermione all my life. I know the old hotel from top to bottom. I have been in all of the apartments, the basement, the laundry, and the restaurant that's been closed for years, and I know about the deserted tennis courts and the second, unused, and hidden swimming pool where the enormous turtle lives. I know things about the hotel that Mr. Glanvill, the manager, does not know. Chase, my favorite ghost, was the one who showed me where to find the master key someone had mislaid a long time ago. It opens every door in the place except the one to Valentino's apartment where all the ghosts hang out, because the door lock is rusted solid.

Chase is not the ghost of a person. She is the ghost of a black bunny rabbit. She has been sort of my own personal ghost since I was a baby. We are able to talk, which is something you can't do with a living bunny. Chase changes size. Usually, she is bunny-size, but I have seen her get to be as large as a German shepherd dog.

Rudolph Valentino is the ghost most people would know about, because he was a big movie star in the 1920s—but the oldest ghost, and the one who should be most famous, really, is La Brea Woman. Valentino doesn't compare to La Brea Woman for being distinguished. She is the only human whose bones have been pulled out of the La Brea Tar Pits. She lived about nine thousand years ago. She is the oldest human ever found in Southern California. Plus, she was murdered—someone knocked her on the head with a rock. We are all proud of La Brea Woman. And she's a nice ghost. She's shorter than I am, in her early twenties, and she always has her hair in curlers and wears sunglasses with pink frames and fuzzy pink slippers. She is friendly and cheerful, and talks a blue streak in some ancient dialect that hasn't been heard on earth in thousands of years.

I don't know exactly how many ghosts live in the Hermione—at least a dozen, maybe more. Not all of them like to communicate—they just haunt, appear and disappear, walk the corridors—some of them moan, or cry, or make ghostly laughter. Chase is the only ghost with whom I can have a conversation. Valentino will exchange a few words with me—but that's just his polite nature. Also, he may be nice to me because he knew my father in the old days.

CHAPTER 2

Hollywood History

My name is Yggdrasil Birnbaum—most people call me Iggy, which I do not like, but what are you going to do? And my father is Captain Buffalo Birnbaum, the old-time cowboy movie star. He is very old for a father—he is fairly old for anybody. He is the handsomest man alive. His story is an interesting one. He was the son of a wealthy family. He was born late in life, as I was to him, to Colonel Horatius Birnbaum, who fought in the Civil War. After the war, Grandpa Horatius went to Chicago and got rich in the glue business.

Everyone has heard of Alpenglue, "the mucilage of mountaineers." It was the first modern superadhesive, and Horatius invented it and made millions selling it to a nation bursting with busted things that needed to be glued during the great westward expansion. No homesteader in a covered wagon or prospector heading for the gold fields would have thought of setting out on the trip without a supply of Alpenglue, to repair broken wagon wheels, or stick the handles back on his six-shooter. Alpenglue could also be used to stitch up tomahawk wounds, and smeared on the bottoms of boots it enabled the wearer to cross frozen mountain passes in winter. And you could eat it if you were starving.

By the time my father and his twin brother, Herman, were born, the days of the Old West were almost over. It didn't last very long. Trains already crossed the country and cities had electric lights and telephones. But there were still bad men and lawmen, some of the old Indian war chiefs were still alive, and cowboys still rode the range. As young men, Buffalo (who was called Buck in those days) and Herman wanted adventure—so instead of going east to college, they took a supply of Alpenglue and their boots and bedrolls and headed west.

My father got to be called Buffalo not because he was a big buffalo hunter—the great herds had already been killed off by the time he got to the West. He got to be called Buffalo because while most cowboy sharpshooters, quick-draw artists, gunfighters, and pistoleros could shoot a silver dollar thrown into the air, he could hit a nickel, which has a buffalo on it—hence the name.

My father and his brother, Herman, who later mysteriously disappeared, had lots of adventures, rode the range, worked in the oil fields, lived with Indian medicine men, prospected for gold, and ran the first combination soda fountain and Turkish bath west of the Rockies, and at one time Herman, who came to be known as Prairie Dog Birnbaum, was the acting governor of Montana. A film director named Max Von Hinten saw my father giving an exhibition of trick riding to entertain some friends, noticed that he was the handsomest man alive, and talked him into coming to Hollywood to act in movies.

It wasn't long before my father was a big movie star. This was in the days before movies had sound. Hollywood was growing by leaps and bounds, and heaps of money were being made. My father had a deluxe apartment at the Hermione, owned a big Italian car completely covered with hand-tooled leather, and kept an African lion as a pet. When talking pictures came in a lot of actors lost their careers because they didn't sound good, but my father continued to be a movie star, only not such a big one. He made some movies in which he played a character called the Baritone Buckaroo. In these movies he was a cowboy who sang. My father couldn't sing, so they had him move his lips and the singing was done by an opera singer named Lauritz Melchior.

By this time, my father was getting a little bored with being a movie star. Also, he was pretty old. He could still ride better than anyone but Roy Rogers, and he was still the handsomest man alive, but he wasn't enjoying being an actor so much. Also, he had saved a ton of money and still had his share of the Alpenglue fortune, so there was really no reason to work. His last movie was called *The Baritone Buckaroo Fights the Nazis*. After that, and to this day, he spends time at our ranch in Arizona, or here standing around Gower Street talking with the other old cowboys, and also hanging out in the History Department at UCLA, helping to record the history of the Old West.

CHAPTER 3

My Mother Has Theories

My mother is much younger than my father. She is sort of a normal age for a mother. She is a psychiatrist. She and my father met when the studio sent him to see her about the morbid fear of horses he had developed. He wasn't so much afraid to ride them, but when he was in bed he would imagine that there were horses in his living room, drinking his liquor and laughing at him. The next day, on the movie set, he would turn suddenly and say to the nearest horse, "So, you think I'm a joke, is that it? You think I'm a figure of fun, do you, you miserable hay burner? I know what you and those other plugs think of me." So the studio sent him to see my mother, and they talked it over. She helped him to understand that his problem arose partly from having grown up in the glue business, and also that the horses probably really were laughing at him for being in those lousy Baritone Buckaroo movies.

My mother is the most beautiful psychiatrist alive, and she looked good with my father driving around Los Angeles in the Bugatti touring car, getting hot fudge sundaes at drive-in restaurants. Pretty soon they fell in love, got married, and had me.

My mother still does psychiatry. Most of her patients are movie stars. She says that Hollywood is a gold mine for a psychiatrist. Because she is a psychiatrist, she has theories of child rearing. Her biggest theory is that stress is bad. She thinks that all ailments, mental and physical, are caused by stress. She thinks stress is worse than the Black Plague or a herd of stampeding bull elephants. I am strictly forbidden to be frustrated, repressed, or restrained. This can be annoying. Sometimes you want to be frustrated, repressed, or restrained. Of course, I am also strictly forbidden to be annoyed. To keep me as stress-free as possible, my mother enrolled me in the Harmonious Reality School.

The Harmonious Reality School is modern, progressive, and advanced. It was started by an avocado grower from the San Fernando Valley named Dr. Nathan Pedwee. He wasn't a regular doctor—he was a fruitopath. Fruitopathy is the science of healing diseases with various kinds of fruit. Dr. Nathan Pedwee got rich selling avocados and real estate, and also wrote a book about how to improve your golf game. His theory about how to become a better golfer was to live a stress-free life. He thought that stress created muscular tension, and that would mess up your swing. Avocados, he said, were the antidote to muscular tension—avocados, and never being made to do anything you didn't want to do. The school runs on his avocados and no-stress principles, as explained in his book *The Pedwee Way*.

You can major in finger painting through sixth grade at the Harmonious Reality School. It is a fully accredited primary and secondary school, recognized by the Department of Education of the State of California.

I like the Harmonious Reality School fairly well. You can do pretty much whatever you want, including getting up and leaving the premises. I do this fairly often. The school is near Sunset and Vine, which is smack in the middle of Hollywood, and there are lots of things to do and look at in the neighborhood. The teachers are polite, and the kids, while confused and mostly illiterate, are friendly.

Needless to say, there's a lot of health food served at lunch, especially avocados, and this guy called Gypsy Boots comes in from time to time to lecture on nutrition. I tend to slip out at lunchtime and get a bowl of chili or a hamburger over on Vine Street.

CHAPTER 4

I Am Not Antisocial

I don't often socialize with the Harmonious Reality kids outside of school. It's not that they aren't nice kids, but they are all . . . droopy. They are too cooperative—they're completely on board with the health food, no-stress, never-compete, avoid-anything-difficult philosophy, and it makes them seem to me that they're missing a part.

I read in *Coronet* magazine, in one of those bottom-of-the-page things, there's an old Spanish saying: "A kiss without the mustache is like an egg without salt." This stuck in my mind. For one thing, if a kiss is like an egg, that's pretty disgusting right there. And if it's like an egg with a mustache, that's beyond disgusting. But it makes a point I can apply to my fellow Harmonious Reality students—they're like eggs without mustaches. I prefer to spend my time with the various characters who hang out in the neighborhood. There are always cowboy actors, extras who pick up work by the day at the movie studios, hanging out around Gower Gulch (that's Gower Street and Sunset Boulevard).

Most of these guys were real cowboys, and they all know my father, so they're nice to me. They lean against the buildings, rolling cigarettes, and spitting, and telling stories about the old days. Of course, every one of them has a secret map to a gold mine that's guarded by Indian spirits or magic rattlesnakes. There are a couple of drugstores where the serious actors hang out and show off for one another. They're not as interesting as the cowboys, but it's fun to watch them, especially when someone like Orson Welles or some other big director comes in for a milk shake and they all try to get him to look at them.

And then there is a nice assortment of street loonies, like the Leprechaun Man, who's always talking about, and to, the Little People, and my friend Chief Crazy Wig, who is a real shaman, I think, and occasionally works as an Indian extra at Columbia pictures.

When I get tired of standing around in the street I can go into the CBS building and talk to the engineers at radio station KNX and look at all the neat radio equipment, or sit in the audience and watch them do a radio show. They have a television station too, but not much goes on there in the daytime. And there's the public library, where I spend a lot of time, reading or talking with the old men and lady bums who sort of live there. Another place I like is the Hindu temple and mushroomburger stand with a nice garden behind it.

As for personal friends my own age, there are these military school kids I spend time with, Neddie Wentworthstein and Seamus Finn. Neddie lives in the Hermione, and Seamus Finn hangs out with Neddie's family most of the time, so he as good as lives here. A couple of years ago, Neddie had us all convinced that the world was coming to an end—the world, or civilization as we know it—and only he could prevent it from happening. Crazy Wig and another Indian shaman named Melvin were in on it. The big crisis was supposed to happen on a certain night, and Neddie went off to have some kind of battle with the powers of darkness.

And that was the last we heard about it. The next day, everything was normal as usual. Neddie said there was nothing to worry about and refused to discuss the details. In fact, the only unusual thing was that it must have rained a colossal amount during the night while everyone was sleeping, because the whole town was really, really soaking wet in the morning. I mean really soaking wet. Stuff was floating.

So I assume Neddie is kind of crazy, or maybe he was just influenced by Crazy Wig and Melvin, who are obviously deranged. Nice guys, though, all of them. Seamus Finn is the handsome son of the handsome movie actor Aaron Finn. He's nice too. I went to his bar mitzvah.

Seamus and Neddie go to Brown-Sparrow Military Academy, which is the complete opposite of Harmonious Reality. They have to wear uniforms, and march, and salute each other. I don't see how they can stand it. And they have a friend who is a ghost! Billy the Phantom Bellboy. He's different from the Hermione ghosts in that they all sort of hang around and haunt one place. Billy used to haunt a hotel in Arizona, but he took off with Neddie and Seamus and now he lives—well, not lives—in Los Angeles, and goes all over the place, wherever he wants. Those are my friends. Call me weird, but I think my best friend is Chase the ghost bunny rabbit.

CHAPTER 5

Cutting School

It's about a hundred times harder to cut school at Brown-Sparrow Military Academy than it is to just walk out of Harmonious Reality. It's a military school. They have rules, and rules, and rules. It may help that the guy who stands guard at the gate, Sergeant Caleb, is Neddie Wentworthstein's shaman friend Melvin. I have seen Melvin at work, in his crisp Marine Corps uniform—apparently he is a genuine retired Marine Corps sergeant—and it's a far cry from the way he looks when he is hanging out at the Rolling Doughnut, where he dresses like a be-bop hipster.

Anyway, on this particular day, I came out of the Harmonious Reality School like a shot at lunchtime, intending to head over to Vine Street and get a tamale. There in the street, wearing their stupid uniforms, were Neddie and Seamus Finn.

"Going to lunch?" Seamus asked.

"Come with us. We're going downtown to Clifton's Cafeteria."

"Is that the gigantic place with the waterfalls, and the fake Polynesian decorations, and the neon palm trees? I've heard about it."

"That's the place," Neddie said. "Also, there's part of the restaurant where there's an indoor rainstorm every twenty minutes, you don't have to pay for your meal if you don't want to, and there are life-size dioramas of scenes from the life of Jesus in the basement."

"I've always wanted to go there," I said. "But how are we going to get downtown and back? We might have to wait an hour for a bus, each way, and it's too far to walk."

"Behold!" Seamus and Neddie said. They stepped aside to left and right and revealed a fancy Packard convertible.

"Isn't that your father's car?" I asked Seamus.

"Yep. We borrowed it," Seamus said.

"Wait! You guys aren't old enough to drive," I said.

"Billy is going to drive," Neddie said.

"Billy? Billy the Phantom Bellboy? He's a ghost. He's dead."

"But I have a license," Billy said. If I squinted, I could just about see him in the driver's seat. Ghosts hardly show up well in daylight.

"Putting aside that you are not among the living, how could you have a license?" I asked Billy. "You don't look any older than maybe fourteen."

"I'm fifty-nine," Billy said. "I was fifteen when I died."

"Wait. You got a driver's license after you were dead?"

"Do you want to stand around in the street talking, or do you want to come with us?" Billy asked. I climbed into the car.

"Are you sure this is all right with your father?" I asked Seamus.

"As you know, Aaron Finn is sort of my employer," Billy the Phantom Bellboy said. "I act as a technical advisor on ghostly matters, and script consultant. Use of the car is one of the fringe benefits, since there's no point paying me with money, me being a ghost and all." He put the car in gear and it lurched forward.

"It looks like nobody's driving," I said. "What if a cop stops us?"

"Billy will show the cop his license," Neddie said.

"That will be interesting," I said.

"Look, there is nothing in the California Motor Vehicle Code that says you specifically have to be alive to drive," Billy said. "And they issued me a license, so that more or less proves it."

"I'm curious. How did that come about, anyway?"

"It's a long story," Billy the Phantom Bellboy said. "Mysterious things happen at the Motor Vehicle Bureau." He switched on the radio. A song was playing, "Nature Boy," sung by Nat King Cole. It had been a big hit a couple of years before. It's a fairly goofy song about this kid who wanders around to no particular purpose.

"I happen to know that this song was written about Gypsy Boots, who comes to my school periodically to tell us about nuts and fruits. And it was the theme song for a very good movie, called *The Boy with Green Hair*," I said.

"And someone wrote a song called 'Serutan Yob,' which is 'Nature's Boy' spelled backwards," Seamus Finn said. "Sometimes Hawthorne plays it on his radio show."

Hawthorne is this crazy disc jockey we all listen to. We pulled up in front of Clifton's Cafeteria, which was the most amazing place I had ever seen.

CHAPTER 6

Pacific Seas

New Hampshire has granite. Indiana has limestone. Georgia has marble. Los Angeles has stucco. Stucco is a cement mixture spread over a wooden framework covered with tarpaper and chicken wire. You can make anything you want, any shape, and cover it with stucco. Clifton's Cafeteria, also known as Pacific Seas, is the last word in stucco gone mad.

The front of the building is all fake rocks made of stucco, and fake tropical plants, so many that it's just a big jumble—or a big jungle. If it were a fun house at an amusement park, I would be afraid to go in. It goes up pretty high, about three stories, and there is a big waterfall coming right down the middle. It is unusual. It is impressive. It is like no other cafeteria. The Los Angeles Architectural Commission wanted to sue them for making a weird eyesore in the middle of the city when they first put it up.

Then you go inside and realize that the outside didn't prepare you for what you see. There are more fake tropical plants, including five palm trees made out of neon tubing, all lit up. There are twelve waterfalls. The whole inside of the restaurant is at different levels, terraces going all the way up, so there are people eating just under the roof, which is pretty high up, and what you see when you look out across the restaurant looks like some big crazy painting. There are plenty of fake stucco rock ledges and overhangs, a wishing well, and a big fireplace. There's a lot of bamboo, and thatched roofs made of dried grass, and phony South Sea carvings and statues. There's the Flower Grotto. There's the Rain Hut, where there's a tropical rain every twenty minutes, and there's a little old lady thumping away on an electric organ.

And there are all these ordinary-looking people sitting in little chairs at little tables, mostly wearing black and dark colors, men in business suits, women wearing hats, knees together, feet together, napkins in their laps, taking little bites, and talking and nodding, just as if they were not part of some colossal wild and wonderful weirdness.

Downstairs, of course, is the Garden of Meditation, with life-size dummies of people in supposedly biblical clothing, and a statue of Jesus in a fake garden of Gethsemane, and live people in biblical robes to explain everything.

The family that owns Clifton's is religious. They are big on the Golden Rule. There is a sign when you come in that says: PAY WHAT YOU WISH—DINE FREE IF NOT DELIGHTED. They give you a bill at the end of the meal, but you don't have to pay it. And you can order the MPM, or Multiple Purpose Meal, which is supposed to be a completely balanced and nutritional meal. It consists of bread, soup, salad, Jell-O, and coffee . . . five cents, or free if you are needy. They started offering the MPM during the Depression, when many people couldn't afford enough to eat, and they still feed a lot of down-and-outers from Skid Row, which isn't far away. We all ordered the MPM, except Billy, who floated over to another table and sniffed someone's Hawaiian ham steak. Ghosts don't eat, but they enjoy sniffing. We all paid our nickels at the end.

We were sitting around the table, sipping our coffee and enjoying our Jell-O, which they offered in every imaginable flavor and color.

"You know," I said, "this is almost precisely the lunch we could have had at our respective school cafeterias, only we wouldn't have had to pay a nickel."

"But this is so much better," Seamus said. "I mean, twelve waterfalls. How can you beat that? Oops! It's raining again!"

We were sitting in the Rain Hut.

CHAPTER 7

Ken Ahara

There was a guy sitting at the next table. He was Japanese, or Japanese American, all decked out in a Joe College outfit, crew cut, tortoiseshell eyeglasses, navy blue sleeveless sweater trimmed in orange, baggy tweed jacket, loafers with white fuzzy socks. He leaned toward us and spoke in a low voice.

"I don't mean to alarm you, but are you aware there's a ghost sitting at your table?"

"A ghost? No fooling?" Seamus Finn said.

"Yes," the college guy said. "And a very unusual one. It is a mobile ghost—that is to say not fixed to a particular haunting place. It is a humaniform ghost, appearing to be an adolescent boy, and it is fairly visible to the trained eye even in this comparatively bright light."

"Remarkable," Neddie Wentworthstein said.

"Astonishing," Seamus Finn said.

"So you know a lot about ghosts?" I asked.

"Excuse me for failing to introduce myself," the guy said. "I am Ken Ahara. I am a postgraduate student in the Ghostology Department at the California Institute of Technology, also known as Cal Tech. I can tell you that this is a very unusual sighting."

"You know, Mr. Ken Ahara, it is rude to talk about someone right in front of one, as if one couldn't hear you, not to mention that you referred to me as 'it,'" Billy the Phantom Bellboy said.

Ken Ahara looked as though he were going to faint. "Oh my goodness!" he said. "It is an interlocutory ghost! It converses!"

"'It' again!" Billy said. "I am a who, not an it. You will notice, Mr. Ken Ahara, that I address you directly. I do not say, 'This graduate student overestimates its knowledge of the spirit world. It finds it unusual to encounter a decent ghost enjoying a sniff of lunch at a fine restaurant.'"

"I do apologize, sir," Ken Ahara said. "It is just that I am very excited. In all my years of study, I have never seen an actual ghost of any kind. If only I had my scientific instruments here, my spectre spectrum chart, my ecto-plasmometer, my infrared camera, my wireless wire recorder! And you, young people! You were aware of the ghost the whole time? And you were not afraid of it . . . of him . . . of him!"

"Why should we be afraid of him?" I asked. "We've known him for years. As to being aware of him, we came with him. He drove us here."

"He . . . drove you here?"

"Well, none of us is old enough to have a license."

"I'm fifty-nine," Billy said.

Ken Ahara was scribbling furiously in a notebook. "Mr. . . . ah . . . Mr.—"

"Call me Billy," Billy said.

"Mr. Billy, I don't suppose I could persuade you to come out to the lab sometime? I'd love for you to meet my professor, Dr. Malocchio, and my fellow grad students."

"No, I'm afraid that would be impossible," Billy said. "You see, it might be a violation of my agreement with my employer."

"Your employer? You work?"

"I have a position in the film industry," Billy said. "I am a technical advisor to the famous actor Mr. Aaron Finn."

"My father," Seamus said.

"So, you see, it might be unethical for me to give you inside ghost information without Mr. Finn's permission. Besides, what's in it for me?"

"There's a stinky cheese lab at Cal Tech," Ken Ahara said.

"Well, that would be of interest," Billy said. "I'll talk it over with Mr. Finn."

CHAPTER 8

The Ghostiest Place in Town

When you grow up around ghosts, right from the time you are a tiny baby, you're used to them. I know some people are scared of them, but they're just ghosts—it's not a big deal. It's not like I am all fascinated with them, and neither do I make a point of ignoring them. They're just part of the atmosphere, like the birds in the trees.

That said, the Hermione is well known to have more ghosts than any other hotel in Hollywood. Most of them have one or two, usually some movie star or other—but the Hermione is practically overrun with them. So it's natural that I would know a certain amount about ghosts and how to get along with them. It's not that I am some kind of spook-o-phile. I try to treat everyone the same, living or dead. I can see why, if you were a ghost, you'd pick the Hermione as a place to live—if you lived. It has all kinds of features of interest. One of the features of interest in our apartment is the stairway to nowhere. Picture an ordinary closet, a hall closet. You open the door, and there it is— a closet. There is a bar going across, and coats on hangers, just like any closet. There is a string hanging down, and you pull the string and a light comes on. Nothing out of the ordinary. But, if you push between the coats, there is a stairway, carpeted, going up, up to the ceiling . . . where it stops.

Obviously, the place was once a duplex, or double-decker apartment, and then the management made it into two apartments and just sealed off the stairs. I find it sort of neat. My parents know there is a stairway there, but they never think about it—they just think of the closet as a closet. So I made it into a sort of extra room for me, a private room. The stairs are nice to sit on. It's a good place to read. And no one ever comes looking for me when I'm there.

Sometimes Chase, my ghostly bunny friend, joins me, and sometimes I entertain on the secret stairs. I can sneak friends in through the coats, and it's cozy sitting on the carpeted steps, maybe passing a bag of cheese crunchies and a bottle of ginger ale up and down. That's what we were doing the day after our visit to Clifton's Cafeteria. Neddie and Seamus were with me.

"So, what was that guy, Ken Ahara, going on about?" Seamus asked.

"Apparently they study ghosts at Cal Tech," Neddie said.

"They ought to come here," I said. "We have ghosts the way some places have mice."

CHAPTER 9

The Penthouse

The Hermione Hotel has a very nice roof. It is all done in terra cotta tile, and there is a little parapet wall all around, so you won't fall to your death. I like to go up there. There's an excellent view in all directions, and usually a nice breeze.

In the middle of the roof there is a stucco structure, consisting of a half-dozen rooms on either side, with doors opening onto a corridor that is open on both ends. It looks sort of like a hotel hallway, or maybe a motel. The rooms are small, about eight foot square, with tiny bathrooms. These were rooms for servants in the old days. People used to travel with their personal maids, or valets, and when they stayed at the Hermione, this was where those servants would sleep. They are the cheapest rooms in the hotel, obviously—and most of them are vacant, except for a few where extremely old ladies live. And also Kitty Nebelstreif.

Kitty Nebelstreif is one of the good things about the Harmonious Reality School. She is the visiting art teacher. Once a week, she comes to give art classes. Of course, art is a big part of the curriculum at Harmonious Reality, and all the teachers, in all the classes, have us kids doing all kinds of painting and drawing and making sculptures out of clay, and papier-mâché, and nailing pieces of wood together— also gluing pasta and seashells and pebbles to hunks of cardboard, and making mobiles out of coat hangers and lengths of yarn, and hanging cutouts, and spools and Ping-Pong balls from them, and everything slathered with poster paint, and sparkles. But Kitty Nebelstreif tells us about things like perspective, and color theory, and vanishing points, and light and shadow, and line and mass and shading, and reads to us from *Lives of the Artists* by Giorgio Vasari. In other words, she is an actual real art teacher.

The rest of the art instruction at Harmonious Reality is more stress-free, free-expression, do-whatever-you-want stuff, and whatever you make, whatever goopy, bloppy, drippy, sparkly thing, the teachers will all say ooh and aah and tell you what a wonderful thing you did. I'm not say-

ing it isn't fun whacking away with great big brushes drip-
ping with thick paint and then sprinkling sparkles all over
whatever it is—but the results get boring after a while,
and there is no way to tell if you're making progress.

Kitty Nebelstreif brings in plaster casts of classical
sculptures and has us try to draw them. Or she takes us
outside and has us try to draw trees and vegetation. It's
hard, and it's frustrating, and stress-making, and it's op-
tional like everything else at the school, so only a few kids
do it.

Kitty Nebelstreif is the aunt of Dr. Nathan Pedwee, the
founder of the school, which is why they even have her
there. She used to work in the art department of one of the
movie studios. When she isn't teaching us art, she is one of
the old ladies waiting to die on the roof of the Hermione
Hotel.

Sometimes I visit her in her tiny room and she serves
me cups of ginger tea, which she makes on a tiny hot plate.

CHAPTER 10

Gone Ghost

Kitty Nebelstreif has lived in the Hermione for years and years and knows everything that goes on. I was visiting her—it was a nice day, and we were having our tea and some of these crescent-shaped almond cookies, the ones with powdered sugar, at one of the wrought-iron tables on the roof—when she said, "La Brea Woman seems to have disappeared."

Of course, Kitty Nebelstreif knew all about the hotel ghosts.

"You mean you haven't seen her lately?" I asked.

"Nobody has. She doesn't seem to be anywhere."

"That's odd," I said. I realized that I hadn't seen the ghost of the only human found in the La Brea Tar Pits for a while myself. "She's usually all over the hotel."

"Just so," Kitty Nebelstreif said. "Something funny is going on."

"Do ghosts take off and go elsewhere?" I asked.

"Except for that Billy the Phantom Bellboy who visits your friends Neddie and Seamus, I've never heard of one who does," Kitty Nebelstreif said.

"Maybe she's just keeping to herself," I said. "Though that wouldn't be like her. She's very friendly."

"It's a mystery," Kitty Nebelstreif said.

CHAPTER 11

Ghostology

As I've said, I am not an expert on what ghosts do and do not do. What I know about them is what I have picked up from being around them. Chase, my ghost bunny friend, said more or less the same thing when I asked her.

"Asking me about the habits of ghosts in general is like expecting someone from Argentina to know the principal crops and exports of Paraguay just because they happen to come from the same continent," she said. "Which are principally cotton, tobacco, and to a lesser extent coffee and sugar cane. Paraguay also exports cottonseed, soybean, peanut, coconut palm, castor bean and sunflower oils. And, now that you mention it, I haven't seen La Brea Woman around for the past few days."

"So what do you think happened?" I asked.

"No idea," Chase said. "But, you know, there are a lot more ghosts here than you have ever seen, or know about. Dozens and dozens of ghosts. It's like a whole town of ghosts. You just see the ones who don't mind being seen. La Brea Woman might have just taken up with ghosts in some other part of the hotel, or maybe she went off visiting, or moved."

"Do ghosts do that?" I asked.

"Again, no idea," Chase said. "Did you know they are cleaning up the restaurant?"

There used to be a restaurant in the hotel, but it was shut down and locked up years ago. Of course, I have let myself in with my master key, and sometimes fix myself a hot chocolate in the kitchen, and do my homework at one of the tables.

"They're reopening it?" I asked.

"Not exactly," Chase said. "What I heard was that Gypsy Boots is going to use the place to give some kind of health food cooking class."

If you want to know what's going on, ask a ghost. They hear everything. It turned out my own mother was behind the restaurant cleanup and the cooking class. She, along with some other mothers of students at the

Harmonious Reality School, had arranged for Gypsy Boots to give a series of lectures and cooking demonstrations, and at the end they were going to cook and serve a health food banquet in the restaurant, and charge a big fee to attend. The profits would be donated to the Harmonious Reality School Parents Association to pay for things like . . . health food cooking classes. It all sounded completely stupid, especially since, as far as I understood it, Gypsy Boots thought you should eat practically everything raw and uncooked.

CHAPTER 12

Ghost Detective

I saw that guy, Ken Ahara, again. He was in the garden of the Hermione Hotel, creeping around in the bushes. He had a sort of box with a shoulder strap attached, and a rubber tube coming from it with a rubber bulb in the middle. It looked a little like the thing in the doctor's office they use to check your blood pressure. He was sticking the end of the rubber hose here and there, and squeezing the rubber bulb.

I walked up to him. He was halfway under a bush. "What are you doing?" I asked him.

"Collecting specimens," he said. Then he looked up.

"Oh! You're the little girl I met at Clifton's Cafeteria, with Mr. Billy."

I just love it when people call me "little girl." "And you're the guy who studies ghosts but never saw one before that day," I said.

"Well, I hope to see many more," Ken Ahara said, standing up and dusting off the knees of his Joe College khaki trousers. "Mr. Billy says this is the ghostiest place he has ever seen."

So, Billy has thrown in with the ghost experts at Cal Tech, I thought. I should have known he would not be able to resist the stinky cheese lab.

"Have you ever seen a ghost here, young lady?" Ken Ahara asked.

I like being called "young lady" almost as well as being called "little girl." "Asking this young *woman* about ghosts is like asking someone from Argentina about the principal products and exports of Paraguay," I said.

"You mean like cotton, tobacco, coffee, sugar cane, and cottonseed, soybean, peanut, coconut palm, castor bean, and sunflower oils?" Ken Ahara asked.

"What is that gimmick you're using?" I asked him.

"It's a sniffer," Ken Ahara said. "Same as the gas company uses. See, there's a gauge on top, and it's calibrated to register any ectoplasmic traces it picks up."

"Picking any up?" I asked.

"Not so far," Ken Ahara said. "I might do better in the

interior of the building, but Mr. Glanvill, the manager, said I may not sniff inside."

"So what do you think of a ghost who suddenly stops showing up in her regular haunting spots?" I asked.

"It's really rare for that to happen," Ken Ahara said. "Most ghosts keep to a fairly regular schedule and stay in one haunting territory, very often one specific spot."

"Is there anything that would make a ghost go away altogether?"

"Well, if it was exorcised, or someone called in a professional de-ghoster. In time past, there was a fair amount of that. People didn't want ghosts around."

"They didn't? Why not?"

"Well, to this day," Ken Ahara said, "people are frequently uneasy with ghosts. I think it may be because they feel ghosts can walk in on them in the bathroom whenever they want."

"Ewwww."

"But they don't take into account that there are always mirrors in bathrooms. Ghosts dislike mirrors."

"That's true," I lied. "They find it unnerving not to be able to see their reflections—makes them feel sort of . . . dead. And if you're a ghost, you can never know if you have spinach stuck in your teeth unless someone tells you.

By the way, my name is Yggdrasil Birnbaum. I'll let you get on with your sniffing."

I left Ken Ahara crawling around under the bushes. Of course, he was all wrong about the mirrors. Rudolph Valentino spends hours looking into one and combing his hair.

CHAPTER 13

Atomic Bomb

There is a regular hotel-type desk or counter in the lobby, but there is never anyone standing behind it. People who live in the hotel just go behind the counter to get their mail out of the little cubbyholes, or to get to the office of Mr. Glanvill, the manager.

The person who does most of the actual work around the hotel is Mr. Mangabay. There are a couple of old ladies who come in and run vacuum cleaners up and down the halls, but he does everything else. He takes care of the gardens, fixes the plumbing and wiring, runs errands, collects packages, picks up and delivers laundry, and does tailoring and last-minute repairs in his little room across from the elevator. The door to his room is always partially open, and you can hear his radio playing, always tuned to a hillbilly music station.

"When They Drop the Atomic Bomb," by Jackie Doll and His Pickled Peppers is a typical song popular on this radio station—it's all about how General MacArthur should drop the bomb on the Communists in Korea.

Mr. Mangabay is an anti-Communist, and an atom bomb fan. There are a lot of those around. Neddie Wentworthstein has a Hallicrafters shortwave radio in his room, which is actually a glassed-in sunporch, and sometimes we listen to hams. Hams are amateur radio operators. They talk to each other about their radio sets, and what other hams in other places they have talked with. It's interesting for about ten minutes.

A lot of the ones Neddie's radio picks up live out in the California and Nevada desert areas and talk a lot about driving out to where they can watch the atom bomb tests. They take their kids, and a picnic basket at night, and watch the sky light up. They say it's real pretty, and say how General MacArthur should drop one on the North Korean commies.

Most adults act like the whole thing, the war and the atom bomb, are normal. At school we have all practiced diving under desks and tables and curling up into a ball with our arms over our heads when a teacher hollers, "Duck and cover!" That's supposed to protect us in case of a bomb flattening Los Angeles.

And, at Neddie's school, which is a military school, all the high school boys can't wait to get into the army and go fight the commies in Korea.

One time, an airplane flew over the city and tossed out thousands and thousands of little pieces of paper. We were running around the schoolyard, trying to snatch them. As one fluttered down above me, and as I reached up to get it I could see that it said "This could have been a bomb," and there was an outline of a bomb printed in red. I'm not sure what the point of that was, except to help me and every kid I know decide that we would probably be blown to cinders before very long, which is too depressing to think about—so we don't, mostly.

CHAPTER 14

The Wolf Makes the Blueberry Strong

"It may never happen," Neddie Wentworthstein said.

"What do you mean? My father says the people in charge of everything, the politicians and the military, have a stone age mentality. They're going to keep making those bombs, and testing them, and finally blow the whole world up so there's nothing left but cockroaches and raccoons."

"Well, maybe that will be okay—if you look at it from the standpoint of a cockroach or a raccoon." Neddie gets this way from hanging out with those shamans, Melvin and Crazy Wig. They are optimistic to a very annoying degree. If you make a solid point in an argument with them, or with Neddie—for instance, if you explain that people tend to be idiots and will sooner or later do something really, really stupid—they will come back with folk wisdom, like "The wolf makes the blueberry strong."

"Isn't that supposed to be 'The wolf makes the caribou strong'?"

"Well, wolves like blueberries a lot too."

So I changed the subject. "What do you hear from your ghost friend, Billy?" I asked Neddie.

"He's been going over to Cal Tech and hanging out in that guy's ghost lab. They're all excited, and treat him really well, 'cause he's the only actual ghost they've ever seen."

"Ken Ahara, the grad student, was here, sniffing around," I told Neddie.

"Probably Billy tipped him off that there are a lot of ghosts in the old hotel," Neddie said. "Did you know that La Brea Woman hasn't been seen for a while?"

"I did! Where do you suppose she is?"

"No idea," Neddie said.

CHAPTER 15

Mushroomburgers

My father has a cream-colored Cadillac convertible with seat covers made of hand-tooled saddle leather, and a set of steer horns mounted on the front. Sometimes he and I drive around aimlessly, listening to cowboy music on the radio. We usually wind up at the mushroomburger place, run by Hindu swamis. I could tell my father was thoughtful by the way he munched his mushroom cheeseburger with hot peppers and curry sauce.

"I've been thinking about my brother, Herman," he said.

"Prairie Dog Birnbaum, who disappeared so long ago?" I asked.

"The very same," my father said, dabbing at his mustache with a napkin. "No one seems to know what happened to him. He just up and vanished one day. I often wonder if he is alive somewhere, or merely dead."

"If he were alive, wouldn't he have gotten in touch with you sometime in the last fifty years?"

"Well, Herman was never much for writing," my father said. "It would not be unlike him to keep to himself unless he had something particular to say. I've asked all the old-timers, the cowboys and Indians, if they ever heard anything about him, but no one seems to know. I would like to find out what became of him."

"Can't you hire detectives? Don't they do that, find people?"

"Pinkerton men? I've had the Unblinking Eye Private Investigation Agency on the case for months," my father said. "They haven't come up with a thing. I've exhausted every resource but one."

"And what is that one?"

"The supernatural," my father said. "Your mother tells me that you have some connections in the spirit world."

"Well, only a couple, really, to talk with," I said. "But I am acquainted with some ghosts."

"Of course, your mother believes it's a delusion, brought on by stress, and as a psychiatrist, she'd know, I suppose—but still, perhaps you wouldn't mind making some inquiries."

"Consider it done," I told my father.

CHAPTER 16

Doughnuts at Dawn

I woke up all of a sudden at the crack of dawn. Completely awake. And restless. I felt like getting out of the apartment. I dressed in a hurry.

My mother was already up, doing her morning yoga.

"I'm going out, Mom," I told her.

"Remember to breathe deeply, dear," she said, breathing deeply herself while in the "confused cobra" posture. A minute later, I was out in the street. It was neat in the street at that hour. The sun wasn't quite up, and there was a soft, foggy feeling. No cars were running, there were hardly any lights in windows, and the streetlights were still on. I breathed deeply.

Then I realized I didn't know what I wanted to do

now that I was up and outside. It was hours until school. I decided I ought to have breakfast. I walked over to Vine Street and headed for the Rolling Doughnut. It was open twenty-four hours, the sign said—but I'd only ever been there at more normal times, never so early or very late. A fresh cruller and a coffee with cream would be just right in the slightly chilly morning air.

When I got there, the place was open all right. I could smell the doughnuts cooking way down the block. I went up to the little window, got my cruller and coffee, and carried them to one of the wooden picnic tables. The place was practically deserted—only one other customer, a boy about my age with a low hairline. He was hunched over a black coffee at one of the tables. Ugliest kid I had ever seen—he had pale, greasy-looking skin, coarse black hair in a flattop cut, pudgy hands, a teensy nose, and a fat face. He was wearing a black turtleneck and sunglasses.

"Mind if I join you?" I asked the ugly kid.

"What difference does it make?" he said. He seemed depressed and proud of it.

I sat down across from him. "Sun's coming up," I said, which was kind of stating the obvious, but it was something neutral to say, just to see if he wanted to make conversation.

"Happens," he said. "Dawn on a doomed world," which was cooler than what I had said.

"You dig sounds?" the kid said.

I wasn't sure what that meant, but I took a chance.

"Um, sure. I dig sounds."

"Dig this," the kid said. He started drumming on the table with his stubby fingers. He drummed fast. There was no rhythm to it, just a lot of thumping on the table. It went on for a while. He was obviously caught up in it. Now and then I thought he was going to stop, but he kept on going, fast and slow, whacking different parts of the table. Finally, he came to the end.

"Know what that was?" he asked me.

"No."

"That was Symphony Number Five by Ludwig Van Beethoven," he said. "That cat knew what was happening."

"That's the first time I ever heard anybody drum a symphony," I said.

"Yeah, well, I'm the only one who does it," he said.

"It was good," I said.

"It doesn't matter," the kid said. "Dig. We're just raccoons on the city dump of civilization."

"I'm getting another cruller," I said.

"Get me one too," the kid said. "You got bread?"

"Bread?"

"Money."

"Oh, like dough! Yes, sure." I went to the window and got two crullers.

"My name is Yggdrasil Birnbaum," I said when I got back.

"Crazy," the kid said.

"What's your name?"

"They call me Bruce Bunyip." Bruce Bunyip stuffed the cruller into his face, getting crumbs all over his black sweater. Then he started drumming again. "You dig Diz?" he asked me.

"Diz? Dizzy Gillespie?"

"Yeah. You dig Diz?"

"I dig Diz."

"Cool. You dig Bird? Charlie Parker?"

"I dig him."

"Crazy. You wanna be my girlfriend?"

"I'll think it over," I told Bruce Bunyip.

CHAPTER 17

Sleepover Mary

I got invited to one of the famous sleepovers thrown by Mary Margaret Finklestein. Mary Margaret Finklestein is a girl at Harmonious Reality. Her father is some kind of big wheel in the movie business, and they live in a big house in Beverly Hills. Naturally, I wanted no part of it, but my mother persuaded me to go. She said I ought to have normal friends, and do normal activities. She said I needed socialization. "You don't want to be maladjusted," she said.

I *do* want to be maladjusted.

So I turned up at Mary Margaret Finklestein's house. Also attending the sleepover were Meg, Madge, and Peggy. Meg and Peggy are Harmonious Realitarians, and Madge is a girl Mary Margaret knows from her bullfighting class.

This bullfighting class I know about. It takes place in the backyard of a music school on Beverly Boulevard. I've seen it. You go down this little alley next to the music school, and there is this dirt yard, all fenced in. There are two of these little short fencelike things at either end of the yard— they're to duck behind to protect yourself when the bull charges you. The bull, in this case, is a set of horns mounted on a bicycle wheel, with handles like a wheelbarrow. Someone runs at you with the wheelbarrow-bicycle-bull-horns thing, and you wave the cape around and dodge the horns. No actual bulls are employed. I asked Mary Margaret if she planned to go down to Mexico sometime and do some genuine bullfighting. She said the bullfighting class was just to develop poise, grace, and confidence. She said that she would never hurt a living bull. I told her it was more likely that the bull would do the hurting.

Madge, Mary Margaret's fellow matadora, had round glasses and braces, and drooled when she talked, so she had to keep sucking spit between words.

Madge got cheese in her braces when we had our first sleepover treat—pizza pie. I had heard of pizza pie because of "That's Amore," the Dean Martin song, which was on the radio all the time, but I didn't actually know what it was. The song says that when the moon hits your eye like a big pizza pie, you're in love, which makes no sense. I always pictured the pizza pie as being something like a cream pie. It's round, but it does not resemble any pie I ever saw—it is not a dessert, it does not contain fruit, it does not have a top crust and a bottom crust. It's more like thin, crusty bread than pie, and it has tomatoes, and cheese! It's served hot. It tastes great! It is, without any doubt, the greatest food ever invented, and I predict it is going to be insanely popular.

"It comes from Italy, and our full-time live-in chef comes from Italy, so he knows how to make it," Mary Margaret said.

We had two pizza pies. One had mushrooms in addition to the cheese and tomato sauce, and one had little slices of spicy sausage. Best thing I ever ate.

CHAPTER 18

Who We Like, and Who We Don't

The next sleepover treat was swimming in the Finklesteins' heated indoor and outdoor swimming pool. This pool is part inside the house, and there's a glass wall at one end, like a huge window, that comes down to within a couple of feet of the water, and the pool connects to another, bigger, part of the pool that's outdoors. There are underwater lights, and at night the whole thing glows. We had to wait a half-hour after our pizza before we could swim, and during this time we sat around the indoor part of the pool, wearing bathing suits supplied by the Finklesteins, and talked.

"Let's talk about who we don't like at school," Mary Margaret Finklestein said.

Here we go, I thought. I was starting to feel very maladjusted—and proud of it. Mary Margaret, Meg, and Peggy counted off a bunch of kids they regarded as dopes, drips, and idiots. Madge, from the bullfighting school, did not know these kids because she didn't go to Harmonious Reality, but she agreed that they sounded like dopes, drips, and idiots. Giggle, giggle, squeal, titter. I was a guest, and had eaten Mary Margaret Finklestein's pizza pie, so I said nothing. The conversation turned to who they did like—all of these were boys. They rated which boys at our school were the cutest, and who they would choose for a boyfriend. Plenty of giggling. This was getting intolerable.

So I said something. "I have a boyfriend," I said.

CHAPTER 19

Center of Attention

I knew that would get them. Well, I didn't know in advance, because I just said it, blurted it out. But telling these goofy, giggly, gossipy rich girls I had an actual boyfriend got their attention in a big way. First, none of them had reached the boyfriend stage yet, or even had talked to a boy in a nonidiotic way, and second, I was present as somebody's good deed and wasn't expected to even speak at this sleepover.

I had noticed during the pizza that, while not actually ignoring me—they did smile at me pleasantly—the other girls did not address me directly, or seem to find anything wrong with the fact that I hadn't said a single word after hello. I was sure Mary Margaret Finklestein had been put up to inviting me—and my mother's hand was in this—she was probably friends with someone in the family, or maybe did psychiatry on them. I was there to help me get socialized. Thus, when I said I had a boyfriend, the effect was dynamic, because it was the first sentence I had spoken, and also because it was about something they were all interested in.

"You have a boyfriend?" Mary Margaret, Meg, Peggy, and Madge asked.

"Yep," I said.

"Really?"

"Yep."

"Who is he? What is he like?" they wanted to know.

"Oh, look!" I said. "It's been a half-hour." And I dived into the pool.

I swam laps for a while. The other girls splashed around. And giggled and squealed.

When I got out of the water, Mary Margaret Finklestein asked me right away, "You don't really have a boyfriend, do you?"

"Sure do," I said.

"So, what's his name?"

"They call him . . . Bruce Bunyip," I said. Now it was their turn to surprise me. They knew who he was! Anyway, Meg and Peggy did.

"Bruce Bunyip! Bruce Bunyip is your boyfriend?"

"Yep. He's my sweetie-pie," I said.

"Bruce Bunyip? Bruce Bunyip?" Meg and Peggy were all excited.

"Who is Bruce Bunyip?" Mary Margaret and Madge wanted to know.

"He's bad!" Meg and Peggy told them. "He's practically a juvenile delinquent!"

This was working out better than I could have hoped. "His father is Sholmos Bunyip. He was the head of International Mammon Studios, and the most powerful man in Hollywood. But then he turned into some kind of recluse—he just sits in his room in his house, which is a replica of a Roman villa, and never comes out."

It turned out that Meg's and Peggy's fathers were big wheels in the movie business, like Mary Margaret's, so they knew stuff like this.

"And Bruce Bunyip runs wild. He goes to Brown-Sparrow Military Academy, but they have no control over him. He does whatever he wants."

"Why does Sholmos Bunyip sit in his room like a hermit?" Madge asked. "Did he go crazy or something?"

"Remember two or three years ago, I think it was, when we had that huge rainstorm?" Meg asked.

"Oh, when everything was soaking wet, and stuff was floating around?"

"Yes, and it rained so much that people's memories

were affected and nobody could remember what had happened in the last twenty-four hours."

"Oh, yes! I remember how wet it was after the rain, but I don't remember the rain," Mary Margaret said.

"Right—that happened to everybody," Peggy said. "Well, it was right after that—Sholmos Bunyip was never seen again, and that is when Bruce Bunyip went wild."

They were talking about the rainstorm that happened the night my probably insane friend Neddie Wentworthstein claimed he was going forth to do battle with the powers of darkness.

This was all pretty interesting. I wanted to know more. But the girls had reached their limit for intelligent conversation. I was going to have to question Neddie Wentworthstein—and I would be on the lookout for Bruce Bunyip, my pretend boyfriend, around the Rolling Doughnut. The rest of the sleepover consisted of playing records, also ice cream sundaes, watching an awful movie that had not been released yet in the family's projection room, and I don't know what else, because I went to bed early and read the *Mad* comic I had brought with me.

CHAPTER 20

Why a Duck?

The Hermione has a nice garden—sort of formal, Spanish, with red tile walks, and hunks of lawn. There are some neatly trimmed shrubs, and lots of flowers. Mr. Mangabay takes care of it. There's a good view of it from our living room windows. I observed Neddie Wentworthstein in the garden, exercising his duck.

Neddie has a duck. Also a parakeet. The duck came as a little yellow duckling at Easter time, and Neddie raised it in his sunporch bedroom. Neddie had taught the duck to follow him around, which is no trick—ducks do that naturally, follow their mothers, and Neddie was the only mother the duck had ever known. More impressive was that he had taught the duck to obey the commands "stay" and "sit" and to come when called. He got the technique out of an article about training dogs in *Boys' Life* and adapted it to duck training. The duck's name is Lucifer.

I decided to go down and talk to him.

CHAPTER 21

In the Garden

"Look! Lucifer can drop on command. Lucifer, down!" The duck flopped onto his belly.

"I'm going to teach him to attack," Neddie Wentworthstein said. "He can be a protection duck."

"I wanted to ask you, what happened that night?"

"To what night do you refer?" Neddie asked.

"You remember—the night you went off by yourself to do battle with the powers of darkness, something like that."

"Oh, yes, that night," Neddie said. "It was wet, I remember. The next day the whole town was drenched. Stuff was floating."

"Everybody remembers that," I said. "But what happened to you, and what did you do?"

"It's funny," Neddie said. "I can't for the life of me recall."

"You don't know what happened?"

"Well, I did know. I wrote it all down in a notebook, but I don't know where it is. I put it somewhere safe and then forgot where I put it. Maybe it will turn up sometime."

"That's it?"

"Afraid so. I do feel like something important happened, but it just slipped my mind. Melvin, the guard at my school, says this sort of thing is normal, speaking in his capacity as an actual shaman."

"Sometimes your choice of friends troubles me," I said. "Speaking of which, what do you know about a kid at your school by the name of Bruce Bunyip?"

"Bruce Bunyip! He's a barbarian, or maybe a savage. He's a monster. It took us about a year to get him to stop slugging people at random! And his father was the most feared and hated man in Hollywood before he suddenly went nutso and became some kind of hermit. Why do you want to know about him?"

"I ran into him at an odd hour at the Rolling Doughnut."

"He keeps odd hours. He just ups and leaves the school whenever he feels like it."

"I do that," I said.

"Yes, but you go to a goofy progressive school where you're expected to do as you please. We go to a military academy. We have about a hundred rules for every one at a school like yours. In Bruce's case it is a holdover from when everybody was scared of his father. Lately he has turned into a hipster. He goes down to the Hollywood Ranch Market at two in the morning in hope of running into Marlon Brando, the big actor. Marlon likes to get fruit in the middle of the night. Sometimes he and Bruce sit on the fender of a parked car and play bongo drums."

"Do you happen to know if he has a girlfriend?"

"Who? Marlon Brando?"

"No, Bruce."

"Are you kidding? He doesn't have any friends, period. Lucifer! Come out of there!" Lucifer had gotten under a bush. Neddie stuck his arm out to the side, then folded it smartly to his chest. "I'm teaching him hand signals," he said. The duck ignored him.

"You knew that La Brea Woman seems to be missing," I said.

"I did," Neddie said. "And Valentino hasn't been seen lately, and some other ghosts, too."

"I wonder what's going on."

"Do you think they died?" Neddie asked.

"Can ghosts die?"

"It's an interesting question. Where would they go?"

"Maybe we should talk to that guy Billy the Phantom Bellboy is spending so much time with," I said. "The one who works at the ghostology lab at Cal Tech."

"Oh, I checked into that," Neddie said. "There is no Ghostology Department at Cal Tech."

"Huh?"

"I think it's time we talked to Melvin," Neddie said.

"Your shaman? We can talk to him, but he's just going to tell us not to get excited, and nature will take care of everything—I think we should talk to Seamus's father."

"Aaron Finn? He's a movie actor."

"He's a man of action."

"Let's talk to Melvin first."

CHAPTER 22

Schmoozing with a Shaman

We found Sergeant Melvin Caleb having a hot fudge sundae with nuts at the Zen Pickle Barrel on Wilcox Avenue. The Zen Pickle Barrel started out as something similar to the mushroomburger place, but the proprietor, a guy named Takuan Soho, added ice cream specialties to the menu, and they got to be more popular than Japanese pickles as served in Buddhist monasteries. They still have the pickles, and things like a butterscotch-pickle sundae, but I have never seen anyone order one.

"Hello, Iggy, hello, Cadet Wentworthstein," Melvin said. "Allow me to treat you to an ice cream or pickle specialty."

I ordered a single scoop of strawberry ice cream, and Neddie chose a double chocolate sundae with chocolate ice cream, marshmallow, and nuts. Neddie is from Chicago and basically has no taste or manners.

Melvin is the guy who stands at the gate at Neddie's school, the Brown-Sparrow Military Academy. He is also the person in charge of military discipline—everybody looking neat and wearing the uniform correctly, marching, saluting, and all that. Neddie told me that Melvin is practically the only person there with actual military experience, although all the teachers dress up in officer's uniforms—most of them are former movie actors. When Melvin is on duty at the school, he wears his incredibly crisp and sharp Marine Corps uniform—when seen around town, he favors shirts in loud colors, wild sweaters, goofy hats, and sunglasses. Melvin is also a shaman, probably Navajo, but it's hard to pin him down on the details.

"I was talking to Neddie about that night a couple of years ago," I began.

"To what night do you refer?" Sergeant Caleb asked me.

"You know—there was some kind of crisis with evil spirits or something. Neddie was supposed to confront some dark power, and the whole future of civilization was at stake."

"Oh, I wasn't there," Melvin said. "I had to go to a bowling tournament with my friend Crazy Wig." Crazy

Wig is another shaman. He talks to himself.

"But you know what happened," I said.

"Not in any detail," Melvin said. "Neddie wrote up notes and was going to give them to me to read. What happened to those notes, Neddie?"

"I lost them," Neddie said.

"Well, I'm sure they'll turn up one day," Melvin said. "And I'm sure you did a good job, seeing that we're all here, eating ice cream, and everything is fine."

"Everything may not be fine," I said. "That's why we wanted to talk with you. It seems a couple of ghosts have disappeared—La Brea Woman and Rudolph Valentino. And we wondered if that was normal."

"Oh, you know about that?" Melvin asked.

"You knew about it too?"

"Well, not about La Brea Woman and Valentino—but a number of well-known ghosts have gone missing. There's Harry Houdini, Fritz, the projectionist from the Vogue Theater, two soldiers from the days of Spanish California, and Rin Tin Tin."

"Gee. And this is not a normal thing?"

"Doesn't seem so very normal to me," Melvin said.

"Does it mean something?" I asked.

"It probably means something," Melvin said.

"Should we be worried?"

"Oh, no," Melvin said. "Definitely do not be worried."

"That's a relief," Neddie said.

"Wait," I said. "Melvin, what if you knew for sure that an atomic bomb was going to be dropped on Los Angeles tomorrow? Would you say we should worry then?"

"Oh, no. Definitely do not be worried."

"So, let me put it another way," I said. "When ghosts disappear, is that a bad thing?"

"It might not be good," Melvin said.

You have to know how to talk to Melvin. "Can you say why it might not be good? Can you say what it means when ghosts disappear?"

"Well, it would depend on why they are disappearing," Melvin said. "If they are voluntarily going away—that might mean something bad. Sort of like animals clearing out when there is going to be a volcanic eruption or an earthquake—something like that. On the other hand, if something is taking them away, against their will—that might be bad too."

"So we should worry."

"On the other hand, it might be something good—one of the first things a shaman learns is that one doesn't have all the answers."

"Shamanism is an imprecise science, isn't it?"

"Except for it being a science, you have that right." Just then I thought how awful it would be if my ghostly bunny friend, Chase, were to disappear, and how I would miss her. I wondered if she had told me all she knew. But where could the ghosts be going?

"Where could the ghosts be going?" Neddie asked.

"No idea," Melvin said. "But if you're curious, this is the perfect week to try to find out."

"The perfect week?"

"Sure. You know what Saturday is, don't you?"

CHAPTER 23

The Day After Halloween

"The day after Halloween?" Neddie asked.

"Yes, but something else besides," Melvin said.

"What something else is it?" we asked Melvin the shaman.

"Before I tell you—I mentioned Harry Houdini earlier. You know all about him, do you?"

"He was a magician on the stage?" I said.

"And an escape artist—the kind who can get out of ropes and handcuffs and things?" Neddie said.

"He was world famous," Melvin said. "He drew huge crowds whenever he performed. Audiences would sit still for an hour, or two hours, while he worked his way out of ropes and handcuffs and a canvas mailbag placed inside a trunk, which was then bound up in chains and padlocks and placed behind a screen. Hundreds of kids worldwide suffocated to death, or at least got nasty rope burns trying to imitate his tricks."

"And people would just sit there waiting for him to get out?" I asked.

"Well, there would be a band playing," Melvin said.

"For two hours?" Neddie asked.

"Sometimes."

"It must have been some good band," I said.

"He would also do things like hang upside down by his feet, and get out of a straitjacket and chains. Or he would be tied and chained up and put into a giant milk can full of water, and have to get out before he drowned."

"At least that would take less than two hours," I said.

"People had a different idea of what was entertaining back then," Melvin said.

"I guess."

"And he had a great and abiding interest in the afterlife. When his mother died, he wanted to contact her—in those days mediums and spiritualists were popular, and people would hold séances, trying to talk to the dead. Houdini went to a few of those, but being a professional magician, he easily saw through the tricks the mediums used to convince people they were getting messages from their dead relatives.

"So, Houdini started exposing mediums. He would arrive in a city and go in disguise to the most popular medium, and then he would do a big exposé in the newspaper showing how they used research and confederates to find out things about people who were coming the séance, and all kinds of magician's illusions to make it seem like there were spirits talking. The funny thing is that after he had done this for a while, the mediums would beg him to expose them, because after he left town their business would quadruple because they had been in the newspaper. Never mind that the story told how they were frauds—people would go to them anyway."

"That's the most interesting thing you've told us yet," Neddie said.

"Isn't it? Anyway, the whole time Houdini was exposing mediums, he was hoping to meet a legitimate one so he could really contact his mother, or just anybody actually dead. He never found one.

"Before he himself died, he had made all kinds of arrangements with his wife and his friends. He was going to try to get a signal to them from the other side. They had code words worked out so no fake medium could claim to have gotten in touch with him, and to this day they hold a séance every Halloween, which is the day he died, and try to get in touch with him.

"Now here's the part I like. He has been a fairly popular ghost around Hollywood for years, and done some quite good haunting—I've seen him myself any number of times in the ghostly parade, always escaping from something or other—but he has yet to show up at one of those séances they hold in his honor."

"And now he's gone missing," Neddie said.

"Yep."

"And this story you just told us has something to do with how ghosts have been disappearing, and Halloween coming up?" I asked.

"Well, no, not necessarily," Melvin said. "I just think it's interesting."

"So, what is it you started out to tell us before you went off into the life and death of Houdini?"

"Oh! Right! Día de los Muertos," Melvin said.

"Beg pardon?"

"Día de los Muertos, the Day of the Dead," Melvin said.

"It's Saturday."

"Isn't that just Mexican Halloween?" I asked.

"No. It's better," Melvin said. "I suggest you go down to Olvera Street and find out all about it."

CHAPTER 24

Ghostly Halloween

Before we could go down to Olvera Street and find out about Día de los Muertos, we had to get through regular American Halloween. Neddie, and Seamus Finn, and I were past the age for trick-or-treat, so Halloween would have been a fairly minor holiday for us. We might have gone to a costume party, with the usual bats and witches decorations, and bobbed for apples—reasonably entertaining, but mostly silly—but we knew about ghostly Halloween.

Now, obviously ghosts are going to take Halloween pretty seriously, wherever they may be, but Halloween in Hollywood—well, the departed just go over the top with it. They make a big effort to outdo the living people. The thing you want to see on ghostly Halloween is the parade.

This is not held on some major thoroughfare, like Hollywood Boulevard or Vine Street. It's on Lafcadio Hearn Avenue, which is quiet, and fairly deserted after all the shops are closed.

This is the one night of the year when there's an exception to the stay-in-one-haunting-place rule. The ghosts are out in force, and in a very playful mood. We'd seen all this before, and wouldn't have missed it for anything.

Lafcadio Hearn Avenue is where you go for Oriental antiques, old and rare books, dried roots and herbs. The shops are in the front parlors of old houses that have been fitted with plate-glass display windows. They have little front yards and gardens—they're not up against the sidewalk. It looks more like an old village than a commercial street.

Seamus and I had corned beef and cabbage at Neddie Wentworthstein's apartment before walking over to Lafcadio Hearn Avenue. Neddie's mother is a good cook. We had corn fritters too. On the way out, we found my father sitting in the lobby of the Hermione, tossing playing cards into an upturned hat.

"Heading for the ghostly parade, daughter?" he asked.

"Yep. Want to come with us?"

"Been lots of times," my father said. "I'm waiting for a

friend of mine from the old days, Fat Antelope. We're going to talk sign language. You have fun, children."

"We will."

"If you should get into conversation with any of the spirits, remember to ask about Prairie Dog."

CHAPTER 25

The Big Parade

We got to Lafcadio Hearn Avenue just in time—it was just getting really dark. There was a pretty good crowd lining both sides of the street, waiting for the parade to begin. Everyone was quiet, whispering if they talked at all. One of the ways the ghostly Halloween parade is different from other parades is there isn't shouting and noise from the audience. And the ghosts in the parade are silent—there are bands that come marching along, playing their instruments, but silently. Even ghosts who typically moan, or scream, or make ghostly laughter in the course of their regular haunting are quiet in the parade. We found a good spot, right at the edge of the sidewalk, and craned our necks, looking down the street, waiting to see the first ghosts in the parade. The streetlights went out. We saw a dull glow at the dark end of the street.

"Here they come!" I whispered.

"Shhh!"

The glow got brighter, and closer. It was the ghosts, glowing ectoplasmically. Then we could make out figures. It was exciting. It was hard not to jump up and down, and we had to clap our hands over our mouths to keep from cheering.

First, as always, was the color guard. It was those three guys you always see in reproductions of the painting *The Spirit of '76* by Archibald M. Willard. There is a kid in a three-cornered hat playing a drum, in the middle an old white-haired guy, also with a drum, and next to him a guy with a bandage on his head, playing a fife. It was just like the picture, only these were the actual guys. We couldn't hear them, but they were drumming and fifing. Just behind them was an American flag, only for the occasion there were little skulls instead of stars. The people on the sidelines took their hats off, or put their hand over their heart as the ghostly colors went by. Neddie and Seamus saluted—it's a school rule that they have to wear their uniforms at parades, and if you're in uniform you have to give a military salute.

Next there was the guard of honor, a Confederate officer with his sword out, and six sharp-looking soldiers who had been killed in the Spanish-American War. Behind them came the grand marshal and after him various dignitaries. Usually the grand marshal of the Hollywood Ghostly Halloween Parade is Harry Houdini, but he wasn't there— so we guessed he really had disappeared. In his place was another favorite of the crowd, former president Theodore Roosevelt. This explained why the honor guard was composed of Rough Riders. Teddy was mounted on a magnificent ghostly horse and was doffing his hat to the spectators. The spectators waved wildly and silently to the presidential spectre.

Next in the parade was the crowd of dignitaries, ghosts like former mayors of Los Angeles, including Don Fernando Rivera y Moncada, lieutenant governor of the Californias, who founded the place in 1781, and various Alcaldes, military governors, and city executives since. A popular ghostly citizen is Benjamin Franklin, who moved to L.A. from Philadelphia a hundred years after he died. Also among the distinguished marchers were Eng and Chang the Siamese twins, Jesse James, Sitting Bull, Rex the Wonder Horse, and the original Lassie. This crowd of bigwigs just walked along, waving to friends in the crowd and looking pleased with themselves.

Next came the United States Marine Corps band of 1891, led by John Philip Sousa, playing silently but showing a lot of style. Then there were assorted haunts, headless ghosts, dancing ghosts, levitating ghosts, amorphous balls of light ghosts, and invisible ghosts that aren't seen but give off a distinct chill, or an odd and eerie feeling as they pass. Two full-rigged ghostly sailing ships were in the parade—the Flying Dutchman's ship and the *Half-Moon*. They floated about ten feet above our heads. We also enjoyed the extinct animals from the La Brea Tar Pits: giant sloths, saber-toothed cats, and dire wolves. And there were tourist ghosts among the regulars, wearing shorts and walking along snapping pictures.

A lot of things one usually looks for in the parade were not present. The ghostly swarm of Rocky Mountain locusts, which is always extremely impressive, was not in the parade this time. The ghosts of circus clowns were far fewer in number than we remembered from previous Halloweens. Billy the Phanton Bellboy was supposed to be in the parade, driving Aaron Finn's Packard convertible with Edgar Allen Poe in the back—but they weren't there. And, we saw only one Conestoga wagon full of pioneer ghosts—there were usually five or six.

And then . . . it was over. We watched the ghostly procession make its way up Lafcadio Hearn Avenue and then disappear. The streetlights came back on. This is not to say it wasn't a great parade. If you had never seen one before, you'd have been impressed. But for those of us who had turned out for it regularly, it was a little disappointing.

"I think I got some great shots," someone said. It was

Ken Ahara, the ghostology student. He had various cameras and instruments in little leather cases hanging from his neck on leather straps. "I'm trying out a new film called Ectochrome."

"Hey, we heard there is no Ghostology Department at Cal Tech," Seamus Finn said.

Ahara said, "I only recently found that out. My professor is just a loony who hangs around the library. I wonder if they'll still give me a degree."

"We also heard that a lot of ghosts have been turning up missing," Neddie Wentworthstein said.

"It's true!" Ken Ahara said. "That's one of the reasons I came here tonight. I haven't seen Mr. Billy for a couple of weeks and was hoping he'd be in the parade."

"So you know something about the disappearances?" I asked.

"It's serious," Ken Ahara said. "The ghosts appear to be fading away like . . . ghosts."

CHAPTER 26

Pumpkin Pie and an Apparition

"Hello, kids. Parade was a little light this year, don't you think?" It was Melvin the shaman. With him was Aaron Finn, the movie actor and Seamus's father.

"Hello, Father," Seamus said. "What did you think of the parade?"

"Well, I am a Teddy Roosevelt fan, so I'm satisfied," Aaron Finn said. "I wish the studio would let me play him in a movie."

We introduced Ken Ahara.

"That must be interesting work," Melvin said.

"I'm just a graduate student," Ken Ahara said.

"I say, who's for a slice of pumpkin pie at Albert Allen's Rite Spot?" Aaron Finn asked. "I bet we can fit everyone into the Packard."

In a little while, we were all jammed into a large booth at the restaurant. "Pumpkin pie, all around, and keep it coming," Aaron Finn told the waitress. "Best pumpkin pie in the city," he said to the rest of us. "And they don't skimp on the whipped cream."

"So, have you seen Billy the Phantom Bellboy lately?" Seamus Finn asked his father.

"No, he seems to have taken off somewhere," Aaron Finn said. "He does that, you know."

"We're worried that ghosts have been disappearing," Ken Ahara said. "It might be something very serious."

"Or then again, it might not be," Melvin said.

"What if it is like rats deserting a sinking ship?" Ken Ahara asked. "What if some inconceivable catastrophe is about to happen, so the ghosts are leaving?"

"Didn't something like that almost happen a year or two ago?" Aaron Finn asked. "It was a rainy night, as I re-call—the dark powers were going to come back. I can't quite remember the details, but you must know, Sergeant Caleb, being a shaman and all that."

"I wasn't there," Melvin said. "I was at the bowling tournament that night."

"I think I was there," Neddie said. "But I forget the details."

"I hope you find that notebook, Neddie," Melvin said. "I'd like to read what happened."

"My mother threw out a huge stack of my comic books, without asking," Neddie said. "She claimed they were a fire hazard. It's possible the notebook was with them."

"That's a pity," Melvin said. "But, never mind."

"I'm worried that the ghosts disappearing has some serious meaning," Ken Ahara said.

"Who wants more pumpkin pie?" Aaron Finn said. "Don't be shy. Eat lots—it's good for you."

"Say, do they serve spirits in this place?" a voice said. We looked around. The booths on both sides of ours were empty. "You know what ghosts eat for breakfast? Ghost Toasties!" the voice said.

"Billy!" Neddie Wentworthstein said. "Is that you?"

"Nobody else but," Billy the Phantom Bellboy said, becoming slightly visible.

"We all thought you'd disappeared," Ken Ahara said.

"You mean like this?" Billy asked, becoming invisible again.

"He means, where have you been?" Seamus said.

"Can't tell you that," Billy said. "Top secret."

"A lot of ghosts have been missing lately," I said. "Do you know anything about that?"

"I know all about it," Billy said.

"Can you tell us?"

"Nope. I'm sworn to secrecy."

"Can you at least tell us if it's something bad?" Ken Ahara asked.

"I can't tell you anything," Billy the Phantom Bellboy said. "Does anyone feel like having a hamburger with grilled onions? I'm in the mood for a sniff." Aaron Finn ordered a hamburger for Billy to inhale over.

CHAPTER 27

The Day of the Dead

*Gente, voy a cantar
un pequeño corrido
de la ciudad de Los Angeles
donde se hacen las peliculas,
y un muchacho, Neddie.
Él era honesto y valiente.*

People, I'm going to sing
a little corrido
of the town of Los Angeles,
where movies are made,
and of a boy, Neddie.
He was honest and brave.

A big magician told him to take this turtle,
sacred to the Indians.
When the time would come
when dark and evil powers
came to subjugate the people,
the guy with the turtle
would save the day.

And Neddie did it!
We don't know how he did it.
Neddie is a hero.
He saved the town.
We salute this brave boy
and also I salute you all
and take my leave.

—"Corrido" by street singer on Olvera Street

Olvera Street is in the middle of the crummy downtown sec-
tion of Los Angeles. It's the oldest part, dating back to the
Spanish colonial days. It's a tourist attraction, with Mexican
restaurants and little stands where you can buy a piñata, or
a sombrero, or Mexican pottery. It smells good, with all the
Mexican cooking, and a couple of the old houses have been

restored to the way they were in the 1800s, and you can go in and see how the people lived back then. We'd all been there, on school trips, or with our parents to have dinner—but we had never been there during Día de los Muertos.

Neddie, Seamus, and I took the bus downtown, and when we arrived things were in full swing. There were lots of people wandering around, and the shops and stalls were selling skulls made of candy, and toy skeletons. There were decorations, tombstones with funny epitaphs, and more skeletons dressed up in fancy costumes, and strolling musicians. There were signboards in Spanish and English, explaining what the Day of the Dead was all about.

It turned out the holiday goes back to the Aztecs. It started in Mexico and is still a big deal there, but it has spread to some other Latin American countries—also the Philippines and parts of the United States.

It happens at about the same time as Halloween, All Saint's Day, and All Soul's Day, but the mood is happy rather than spooky. The living people celebrate the lives of the dead and decorate their graves with orange marigolds, also known as *flor de muerto*, or "flower of the dead." The whole thing is upbeat and happy, and there are toys for dead children, aka *los angelitos*, or "little angels," bottles of tequila for dead adults, candy left for the dead, and little trinkets. At home,

the people make shrines and offer candied pumpkin, and
pan de muerto, or "bread of the dead," and make those
sugar skulls with the names of dead friends and relatives
decorating them. The idea is to invite the dead into the
homes so they can enjoy the "spiritual essence" of the
food—I suppose they sniff it, like Billy the Phantom
Bellboy does. They also put out pillows and and blankets
so the dead can have a rest. And they write funny epitaphs,
and make funny dressed-up skeletons, and draw funny car-
toons of funny dressed-up skeletons.

What I got from reading all the signboards and observ-
ing all that was going on was that the dead love a good
party, and on Día de los Muertos, everybody makes sure it's
the best one possible.

What I liked best were the little mariachi bands,
usually two or three guitars and a trumpet, maybe an ac-
cordion. They walked around playing, and would stop and
play for people, and sing these Mexican hillbilly songs. The
musicians all had Mexican cowboy suits, and big som-
breros, and had bushy mustaches. They were great, and
they seemed to be having the most fun of anybody.

Except this one band—the Mexican guys looked
slightly bugged. It was also the only band that had a bongo
player, and the bongo player was Bruce Bunyip! He had a
set of bongo drums hanging from his neck on a string, and

a cheap souvenir sombrero he had bought, or probably stolen, from one of the stands. He was drumming up a storm, but what he drummed didn't necessarily go with what they were playing. You could see the band wished he would go away but weren't sure of how to politely get rid of him.

"Bruce!" I said.

"Babe!" he said. "Did you come down here to hear me make the scene with these Mexi-cats?"

The mariachis took advantage of Bruce's stopping to talk with me to move away, swiftly.

"You sure were doing a lot of drumming," I said.

"They're a little square, but I showed them a few things," Bruce said. Then he saw Neddie and Seamus. "Hey, man! Hey, man! Are you taking care of my chick?" Meaning me.

"She's your chick?" Neddie asked.

"What can I say? The babe digs me," Bruce Bunyip said.

"Amazing!" Seamus Finn said.

"Fascinating!" Neddie Wentworthstein said.

"Oh, crud!" I said.

"You like him?" Seamus asked me.

"I'm ambivalent," I said.

CHAPTER 28

That's It?

"So what was it that Melvin expected us to learn at the Día de los Muertos celebration?" Neddie asked. We were having crullers and coffee at the Rolling Doughnut, our usual Sunday-morning hangout.

"That the dead love a good party?" Seamus guessed. "What does that tell us about ghosts disappearing? Isn't that what we were asking him about?"

"But are ghosts really disappearing—I mean, permanently?" I asked. "We thought Billy had vanished, but he turned up at the restaurant the other night."

"Yes, and he knew about the disappearing ghosts but refused to tell us anything," Seamus said. "Said he was sworn to secrecy, and we couldn't drag a single word about it out of him."

"So something is going on, and he knows what it is, but we can't find out," Neddie said. "And if Billy won't talk, I don't see much chance for finding out—I mean, he's sort of our personal ghost. He's our friend."

"We could ask Melvin to clarify," I said.

"Yeah, right," Neddie said.

"Oh, sure," Seamus said. "You've heard Melvin clarify. He just makes things muddier and muddier."

"Well, I'm going to get to the bottom of it," I said.

"Good luck," Neddie said.

"You'll just be chasing your tail," Seamus said. "It's one of those ghostly secrets—you can't find out a thing."

"Care to make a little wager that I can't find out?" I asked.

"Okay. If you find anything out, we'll pay for your crullers for two months—when you give up, and you will, you have to buy us each crullers for a month. Fair?" Neddie asked.

"Perfectly fair," I said.

They have their ghost, and I have mine, I thought.

CHAPTER 29

Mr. Wentworthstein

Neddie's father is the Shoelace King. When you buy shoelaces, if you look at the little paper wrapper, nine times out of ten it will say WENTWORTHSTEIN SHOELACES. So they are incredibly rich. Mr. Wentworthstein likes saying that he started his fortune on a shoestring—he works it into every conversation.

Mr. Wentworthstein does projects. One of his projects was having scientists develop a shoelace that can't be broken. It took a year, and a huge sum of money, but they came up with one—only it was half an inch thick. Not ready for the marketplace, Mr. Wentworthstein said. Another project was a toy that was supposed to become a huge fad, like the yo-yo—it was called the Shoe-la Hoop, and it was sort of like a lasso, and also a hoop you could swing around your head, and sort of dance and gyrate inside of. He got all of us kids to learn how to play with it, which was hard to do—also, it was boring. He had thousands of them made and got them into stores. Nobody bought even one. Mr. Wentworthstein's current project is the Museum of the Shoelace. Neddie's mother had made a big basketful of corn muffins, and Seamus Finn and I had been invited to help eat them. While we slathered butter and strawberry jam on the muffins, Mr. Wentworthstein told us about the Museum of the Shoelace.

"Before I can open the museum, I have to assemble the collection," Mr. Wentworthstein said. "I already have several exhibits that will be sensational."

"Oh, Father, no one will be interested in seeing shoelaces," Eloise said. Eloise is Neddie's sister, who is older and is going to be an actress.

"On the contrary, daughter," Mr. Wentworthstein said. "People will flock to my museum. They will come by the thousands. For example, I have a shoelace which I am pretty sure belonged to General and later President Ulysses S. Grant. Now, that by itself is a crowd-getter. But it gets better. I have shoelaces that belonged to an ancient Roman emperor, Caligula's Ligula. I have a pair of shoelaces made by South American Indians from the skin of the electric eel—they still have a faint electric current, and we are going to fix it so they light up a tiny lightbulb. I have shoelaces that belonged to Lord Buckley. They are plaid. And of course, the longest shoelace in the world, a scale model of New York City made entirely of shoelaces, an exhibit of shoelaces of the future, in which you will see the twenty-first-century methods by which shoelaces will be manufactured, and simulated spun glass, titanium, and carbon fiber shoelaces. I have a playable violin with shoelace strings and a shoelace bow. And, there will be occasional exhibits with live animals and people—for example, I will have Mongolian tribesmen in the museum, weaving the traditional shoelaces of their people and answering questions from the public. Now, think of it, children—can you imagine a more exciting museum?"

"These are wonderful corn muffins, Mrs. Wentworthstein," Seamus Finn said.

"Yes, they are, Mother," Neddie said. "No one makes corn muffins like yours."

"There is only one thing missing to make my museum a complete success," Mr. Wentworthstein said. "It is the Devil's Shoestring, the rarest shoelace of all."

"Isn't the Devil's Shoestring a natural wonder, a rock formation or some such thing, in Yosemite or some other national park?" I asked.

"It is also a shoelace," Mr. Wentworthstein said.

"What is it like?" Neddie asked.

"I don't know," said Mr. Wentworthstein. "I just know it is the ultimate shoelace collectible. If any of you children ever hear word of it—what it is, where it is, anything—I hope you will tell me promptly.

"We'll be on the lookout for it," we all said with our mouths full of muffin.

CHAPTER 30

Muffins on the Roof

Mrs. Wentworthstein gave me some muffins wrapped in a napkin to take to Kitty Nebelstreif up on the roof.

"These look yummy," Kitty Nebelstreif said. "May I fix one for you? I have some pineapple mango marmalade."

"No thanks," I said. "I am chock full. If I ate another muffin I would fall dead."

"Well, you'll have a cup of blueberry tea," Kitty Nebelstreif said. "Tell me all the news of the outside world."

"Well, this disappearing ghost business has been on my mind," I said.

"They've been clearing out," Kitty Nebelstreif said. "I think half the ghosts are gone from this hotel. I've been getting some good nights' sleep for the first time in years."

"They used to come up here at night and make noise?" I asked.

"Always," Kitty Nebelstreif said. "Ghosts love a good party."

"And you have no idea where they are going or why?"

"Not a clue," Kitty Nebelstreif said. "Mmmmm, these muffins are wonderful."

"Billy the Phantom Bellboy turned up," I said. "I saw him after the ghostly Halloween parade."

"Oh, isn't that fun?" Kitty Nebelstreif said. "I used to go all the time. Did Billy have anything to say about the ghostly disappearances?"

"He said he knew all about it but couldn't tell us a thing. Said he was sworn to secrecy."

"But you plan to find out all about it," Kitty Nebelstreif said.

"You know me well," I said.

CHAPTER 31

Gypsy Boots

"I understand the cookery class is going to happen," Kitty Nebelstreif said.

"The one where the mothers from my school are going to take health food lessons from Gypsy Boots?"

"Yes, the hotel has cleaned up the old restaurant and moved chairs into the kitchen, where Gypsy Boots will demonstrate recipes."

"I thought Gypsy Boots believed in eating everything raw," I said.

"I suppose he is going to show the mothers how to chop things up and put them in a blender," Kitty Nebelstreif said. "Or show them how to chop things up and make them into salads."

"Hardly sounds like a cookery class to me," I said. "More like a chopping class."

"I'm sure it will be very nice," Kitty Nebelstreif said.

"Are you planning to attend yourself?" I asked her.

"No."

I think I have already mentioned that the popular song "Nature Boy" was written about Gypsy Boots. He was the first person to make "health food" widely popular. At one time, he and a bunch of other maniacs lived up in the hills, eating things they found growing wild, wearing hardly any clothes, and sleeping in caves and trees. He invented the "smoothie," which is a bunch of fruits and juices spun in a blender. These blenders are a big item lately. They are sort of like the milk shake machines in soda fountains, only instead of the motor on top and the blades coming down into a big container, blenders have the motor underneath and the blades at the bottom of a tall, thick glass. Everybody buys them, mostly so they can make milk shakes and malteds at home, which are never as good as the ones at the drugstore.

Gypsy Boots is a nice man, and he will stop to talk to anybody about wheatgrass, and why garlic is good for you.

FLOWER AND VEGETABLE SALAD

2 cups thinly sliced cucumber

1 cup chopped onion

1 cup chopped bell pepper

1 cup tomatoes (small pieces)

3–4 minced or chopped nasturtium leaves

Mix all ingredients in a salad bowl, using chopped green nasturtium seed pods instead of leaves if you prefer. If the salad is not moist enough, you may add a teaspoon of safflower or soy oil.

That's one of his. It was in the newspaper.

CHAPTER 32

Talking to a Dead Bunny

I found Chase sniffing some nasturtiums near the deserted and overgrown tennis court behind the hotel. She was about the size of a medium-to-large cocker spaniel on this particular day.

"You know, those are okay to eat," I said. "I just read a recipe in the newspaper."

"Tell me something I don't know already," Chase said. "I'm a rabbit. I know what's what."

"How about you telling me something?" I said.

"Such as what?" Chase asked, moving over to sniff some wild parsley.

"Such as what is the deal with the ghosts disappearing? Where are they all going, and why?"

"You don't know?" Chase asked.

"If I knew, why would I ask you? Billy the Phantom Bellboy claims to know all about it but says he can't tell. Been sworn to secrecy."

"Billy the Phantom Bellboy doesn't know what he is talking about," Chase said. "It's no secret. The ghosts are going down below to enjoy the big event."

"Down below? Big event?"

"Do you know about Walpurgisnacht?"

"You mean Walpurgisnacht, or Walpurga's Night, also known as Hexennacht or Witch's Night, in German? It's an old pagan festival that later got hooked up with the birthday of a saint named Walpurga, and it's supposed to be when all the witches and ghoulies and goblins come out and have a big whoop-de-doo on a mountain called the Blocksberg, also known as the Brocken, which is the highest peak in the Harz Mountains. Is that what you mean?" I asked.

"How do you know so much?" Chase asked.

"I have volume V–W of the *Children's Encyclopedia* in my room," I said. "In Sweden the holiday is known as Valborgsmassoafton or Valborg, which is the Scandinavian name for St. Walpurga. In Finland it's Vapunaatto, and in Estonia it's Volbriöö. People, especially students, have bonfires, and dance outside and drink too much. And it comes exactly six months before or after Halloween to the day. So why are all the ghosts leaving to go to it when Halloween is barely past?"

"I didn't say ghosts were going to it. I just asked if you knew what it was."

"Which I do," I said.

"Which you do," Chase continued. "And I only brought it up as an example of a big supernatural wing-ding. You know, ghosts love a good party."

"And there's going to be one."

"Yes."

"And it's down there, you said."

"Yes. Down there."

"In the Underworld."

"Not exactly."

"In hell."

"Well, no."

"In a big hole in the ground."

"Technically, yes."

"There's going to be a big supernatural wing-ding in a hole in the ground."

"Not really. The wing-ding is on top of a mountain."

"And this mountain is . . ."

"Down there."

"And it's called?"

"What, the mountain?"

"Okay, yes, what is the mountain called?"

"It's called the Devil's Shoestring."

"Interesting. And where is it located? Don't say down there."

"Hackensack."

"Hackensack? That's in New Jersey!"

"This is a different one. And it's called Old New Hackensack. There are worlds within worlds."

"And in Old New Hackensack there's a mountain called the Devil's Shoestring."

"It's tall and skinny."

"And this is where the supernatural hootenanny is going to happen."

"On the mountain, and in the vicinity."

"And all the ghosts are going there."

"Yes."

"Can I go to this party?"

"I suppose, if you knew where it was."

"You just told me, Hackensack, but not the one in New Jersey."

"That's right, Old New Hackensack."

"So I could go?"

"If you knew how to get there."

"How do I get there?"

"Can't tell you. Sworn to secrecy."

"How to get there is a secret?"

"Yes."

"So Billy the Phantom Bellboy was right."

"Just about how to get there—the rest anybody can know."

"Are you going?"

"Probably."

"But you won't take me with you."

"You know, you should follow me around someday. You'd enjoy seeing all the stuff I get up to."

"I'll make a point of doing that," I said.

"Good. I'm sure you'll learn things."

CHAPTER 33

Invitation to Insanity

"Melvin wants to treat us to a meal at Clifton's!" Neddie Wentworthstein said. "It's Crazy Wig's birthday. It will be you, me, Seamus Finn, Crazy Wig of course, Aaron Finn the movie star, Al from school, and Billy the Phantom Bellboy."

This was perfect. "This is perfect," I said. "I have something interesting to discuss with all of you." Al from school is Al Crane, one of the military school kids. He hangs out with Neddie and Seamus, but not all the time. His father is the manager of the Gibbs Brothers Circus, and frankly, he usually has better things to do.

"Everybody has to bring a suitable present, and you can't order anything over five cents—but the restaurant provides a free cake if it's a birthday party," Neddie said. "Doesn't it sound like fun?"

"Actually, it sounds like someone is going to entertain eight people for thirty-five cents—since the ghost doesn't eat—and get a free cake and presents out of it, but I will attend, noting that I appear to be the only female any of you know and the occasion would be drab without me."

"Melvin could invite your boyfriend, Bruce Bunyip," Neddie said.

"I never said he was my boyfriend," I said.

"He says different," Neddie said.

I had not run into Bruce Bunyip since I met him bongo-ing on the Day of the Dead, but I had attained some status at the Harmonious Reality School once word got around that I was stepping out with practically a criminal. I did nothing to discourage the rumor. Apparently, Bruce Bunyip had been doing something similar at the Brown-Sparrow Military Academy. Oh, what a tangled web we weave, when first we practice to deceive.

CHAPTER 34

Loopy Birthday to You

Neddie brought Crazy Wig a pair of fluorescent pink fuzzy shoelaces. Seamus brought him a petrifed possible wolf's tooth. Al gave him a pair of tickets to the circus. Aaron Finn gave him a pair of swordsman's gloves he had worn in some movie. I gave him the latest edition of *Mad Comics*. Melvin gave him argyle socks. Billy, being a ghost, didn't have anything material to give him, but he told him the location of some buried Spanish gold coins. Crazy Wig seemed pleased with his presents. He had on a nice suit and the buffalo-skin hat with horns he always wore, and also a hand-painted necktie with a hula dancer and a palm tree on it.

We had a good table in one of the grottos, with plenty of stucco sculptures looking like those Easter Island heads, and a neon palm tree nearby. We all had the five-cent Multiple Purpose Meal—whole wheat bread, vegetable soup, salad with your choice of dressing, Jell-O in all known flavors, and all the coffee we wanted. The management of Clifton's sent around a tiny cake, just big enough for each of us to have a thin slice, and some Clifton's employees in biblical robes stood around and sang "Happy Birthday." Crazy Wig said it was the best party he'd ever had. While we were sitting around drinking coffee and licking cake crumbs off a fingertip, I decided the right moment had come.

"Neddie and Seamus, you remember our wager. I will be collecting free crullers from you every Sunday for the next two months."

"What's this?" Aaron Finn said. "You children had a wager?"

"They bet me I couldn't find out anything about the recent disappearance of so many ghosts," I said. "Naturally, I found out plenty."

"Impossible!" Billy the Phantom Bellboy said. "That stuff is top secret."

"All the same," I said. "I know what I know."

"All right, Miss Smartypants," Billy the Phantom Bellboy said. "Tell what you know, and I'll tell you if you have it right."

"To begin with," I said, "the ghosts are all going to Hackensack."

"Hackensack? In New Jersey?" Aaron Finn asked.

"It's a different Hackensack. And this one is Old New Hackensack," I said. "Apparently there are worlds within worlds."

"What does that mean?" Al the circus boy asked.

"It means that this plane of existence, where we are now, is not the only one," Melvin the shaman said. "While we are sitting here, digesting our wonderful meal, in the same space and almost the same time, there may be others, fishing in a river, or sleeping, or sawing lumber, walking around—we can't see them, and they can't see us."

"Except sometimes in certain kinds of dreams," Crazy Wig said. "Also, there are portals—places where barriers between the various planes of existence don't exist and you can pass from one to another. And in some cases, where there are old cities, with other older cities buried underneath them, those old cities may not be defunct. They may be going strong, only of course on other planes of existence."

"I think I read something about this in a book," Seamus Finn said. "Some fiction about a boy from Mars."

"I don't know a lot about that," I said. "But I do know that there is going to be a big hootenanny of some kind in the not-in-New-Jersey Hackensack, and ghosts, who love a good party, are all heading there. How am I doing, Mr. Phantom Bellboy?"

"How did you find all this out?" Billy asked.

"I have my methods."

"What do you two shamans say?" Aaron Finn asked Melvin and Crazy Wig. "Is young Yggdrasil telling us the emmis? Is there a non-New-Jerseyan Hackensack on another plane of existence?"

"Sure," Crazy Wig said. "Been there lots of times."

"Lots of times," Melvin said.

"So the crullers are mine," I said to Neddie and Seamus. "See that you pay up. And I will tell you something else, free and for nothing. I am going to that party."

CHAPTER 35

This Is the Plan

"We're going with you," Neddie Wentworthstein said.

"To the hootenanny in not-in-New-Jersey Old New Hackensack?" I asked.

"Yes, the hootenanny, or hauntenanny, or walpurgisenanny, or whatever it is. If you're going, we want to go too," Seamus Finn said.

We were sitting on the secret closet stairs to nowhere, drinking Dr. Pedwee's cream soda and sharing a bag of Gypsy Boots's whole-grain cuchifritos.

"If you want to come along, then come along," I said. "But it should be understood—we don't know where we're going, and we don't know what will happen. I don't want any crybabies on this trip."

"You wrong us," Seamus Finn said.

"Didn't I protect civilization from . . . um . . . something bad?" Neddie Wentworthstein said.

"We think you may have," I said. "It would be more impressive if anyone, including you, remembered it. But, I apologize for the crybaby remark. I can't think of two better companions for a trip into the unknown. You, Seamus, are the son of a movie star famous for swordfights in practically every movie—you must have inherited some of that style."

"And Neddie is a junior shaman of some kind," Seamus said. "That may come in handy. Also, he has a magical talisman."

"Oh, yes, the turtle. You have that with you, Neddie?"

"At all times," Neddie said.

The turtle is a little carved stone one that Melvin the shaman gave Neddie when they first met. It's supposed to be important in some way.

"So what is the plan?" Neddie and Seamus wanted to know.

"Well, we know where we want to go," I said. "Apparently there is some kind of invisible world everybody seems to have known about except us . . . Melvin and Crazy Wig, all the ghosts. The part no one seems willing to tell us—anyway, tell us outright—is how to get there. But Chase gave me a strong hint."

"Chase, your ghostly bunny friend?"

"The same. She refuses to tell me where the portal to this other world is, but she suggested I follow her around and see where she goes. I think she means to make a move, and go through some kind of magic doorway that connects this plane of existence with the one that contains Old New Hackensack."

"And when you see where she goes . . ."

"We'll know how to get in."

CHAPTER 36

Wiener Whistles

We decided to spread out through the hotel and watch for Chase. To signal one another, we had Oscar Mayer Wiener Whistles. Seamus Finn had left his in his room at the military school, but I had two, so loaned him one of mine. These are whistles you get for free when the Oscar Mayer Wienermobile comes around. It is a car shaped like a hot dog, and there is a little person dressed as a chef who hands out the Wiener Whistles. They are shaped like a hot dog too, and make a nice hollow hooting kind of sound. The idea was that if any of us saw Chase, we would toot our Wiener Whistle, and the other two would head for the sound.

"Won't that alert Chase that she is being watched?" Seamus Finn asked.

"If I understood what she said to me, she expects to be watched. She wants to tell me where the secret entrance to the secret world is, but she can't come right out and just say it. Some kind of ghostly rule, I guess. So I am betting she will ignore the whistle and just go about her business. Toot softly, and every few seconds, so the others can find you."

We spread out. Neddie took the upper floors, Seamus took the middle ones, and I took the lower stories of the hotel, the lobby, and the basement. It wasn't long before I heard a faint tooting coming from above. I raced up the stairs. The tooting was getting clearer. I passed the middle floors, with no sign of Seamus Finn, and when I reached the second-to-the-top-floor hallway, both boys were there.

"Where is she?" I asked.

"She was here a minute ago. Now she's disappeared again."

"Spread out again."

We spread out. It would have been much better if we had walkie-talkies or some kind of two-way radios for this. Then I heard tooting from above—it was Seamus this time. I raced up and Neddie raced down. Again, Chase had disappeared by the time we assembled.

There were a few more false alarms, and sightings of Chase scurrying through the corridors only to vanish before we could all converge.

"Chase covers a lot of territory in the course of a day," Seamus Finn said.

"She's a busy bunny," I said.

CHAPTER 37

Through the Cooking Class

We were all on the ground floor of the Hermione, in the utility area behind the lobby—I had seen Chase in the vicinity of Mr. Mangabay's room. The door was partly open, and Mr. Mangabay was inside, ironing and listening to anti-Communist hillbilly music.

"Wait! There she is again!" Neddie said.

"She's heading for the old restaurant," I said. We hurried down the corridor after her. Chase went into the former restaurant, now made tidy and set up for Gypsy Boots's health food cookery lessons. We saw Chase make her way into the kitchen and then squeeze through a little door standing ajar at the very back.

"What do we do now, just crowd in after her?" Neddie asked.

"Better let me go in first," I said. "She and I are friends."

I slipped through the partially open door and found myself in a little room not much bigger than a closet. It was fairly dark—I could barely see anything, but I could see I was alone—Chase was not present. The little room was empty, the walls were of tile, and there was a small iron door, over which there was a sign: BOMB SHEL-TER. I tooted my Wiener Whistle a couple of times, and Neddie and Seamus appeared.

"Where's the bunny?" they asked.

"As you see," I said.

"Could she have opened that iron door? It looks heavy."

"She's a ghost. She could have passed right through it."

"Well, we're not ghosts. Let's see if we can open it."

"Bomb shelter. I know about those. In case of an atomic attack, you come down here and there is food and water—enough to keep you alive until it is time to go outside and see the total ruination of the city, everybody dead, and huge mutant monsters, pets like white mice turned into gigantic killers by the radiation."

"Help me get this thing open," I said. We pulled the iron door open. Another little room, this one was almost totally dark.

"Look! Here's a candle and a box of matches," Seamus Finn said. He lit the candle and we saw a steep flight of iron stairs leading down. We descended. There were iron cots, big cartons marked SURVIVAL CRACKERS and DEHYDRATED SOUP, and big cans marked DRINKING WATER.

"This is spooky," I said. "I can imagine people sitting down here for weeks and months and going nuts."

"And listening to the giant mutant white mice scratching at the door, trying to get in and eat them," Neddie said. "I wonder what this button is for." Set into the wall was a brass plate with a large red button in the middle. Under the button were letters that spelled out DOWN.

"Don't push . . ."

Neddie pushed it. The iron door slammed shut, creating a gust of air that blew out the candle. The room began to vibrate and shake. We heard grinding mechanical noises, and had the sensation of sinking.

". . . it!" I said.

"No, probably shouldn't have," Neddie said. The grinding noises and vibrating continued, and the feeling of sinking turned into a feeling of falling. You felt it in your stomach.

Seamus Finn was scrambling around, trying to find the candle and strike a match. When he got it lit, everything looked the way it had, except our faces, which looked sick. "You know what this feels like?" Neddie asked.

"Elevator?"

"Yes!"

Just then there was a bump. The falling feeling stopped, and the door popped open. Bright sunlight flooded in. We practically climbed over one another scrambling up the stairs and popping through the popped-open door. Having popped out, we tumbled a foot or two and found ourselves lying on green grass.

"What the heck?" Seamus said.

"We're in some kind of a meadow!" Neddie said. "Look! There goes Chase!" I said. Chase was scampering off in the direction of some bushes. "So we're there?" Seamus asked.

"I don't know. I guess we are."

"So how come there's a sun and sky and clouds and all, if we just descended, as I am assuming we have, into the bowels of the earth?" Neddie asked.

"I always wondered about that when Alice went down the hole after the white rabbit," I said. "You'd think it would be some sort of cave or cavern."

"I wondered that too," Seamus Finn said. "We just did more or less the same thing as Alice, didn't we?"

"Pretty much," I said. "Only our rabbit is black."

"So the parallel-worlds thing Melvin and Crazy Wig were talking about is right?" Seamus asked.

"This raises some questions about astronomy and physics," Neddie said. "I mean, is the sun shining on us now the same sun we're used to? Is this the same solar system we live in every day? And if the bomb shelter descended like an elevator, into the earth, then aren't we inside the earth? Or . . . were our senses fooled, and because the button I pushed—"

"We probably should have talked that over before pushing it," Seamus said.

"Agreed," Neddie said. "Anyway, what if because the button was marked 'Down,' when the bomb shelter began to shake around and make noises, we assumed it was descending? What if it was actually taking off like a rocket? What if instead of being inside the earth, we're on some other planet? Or, according to the Melvin and Crazy Wig idea, what if there are all these different planes of existence all existing in the same space, and it didn't go anywhere, just shook around and vibrated and made noises, and then we popped out in the same physical place, and the place we're in overlaps the space where the Hermione Hotel stands, but before we were seeing only that space and now we can see only this other one?"

"Interesting questions," I said. "Here's another one. Do you see the door we just popped out of? Where is the bomb shelter?"

"Hmmm. That *is* interesting," Seamus Finn said. "It's nowhere in sight. There may be a problem getting home. What do we do now?"

"Let's keep following Chase," I said. "She looked as though she knew where she was going."

CHAPTER 38

Iggy in Underland

"I don't see Chase. Where is she?"

"She was heading for those bushes."

"Let's go after her. Run!"

It occurred to all of us at the same moment that Chase was the only one who could possibly tell us how to get back from wherever we were. As we ran across the huge meadow, we were realizing that it was not out in the country but was some kind of park set in the middle of a city. All around the meadow part of it was shrubbery and trees, and outside it were streets. We could see the tops of buildings and houses over the treetops in some places.

"If Chase gets out of here and into the city, how are we going to ever catch up with her?" Seamus said, puffing as he ran.

"Good question," I said, also puffing.

We were getting close to the edge of the park. We could see buses, cars, and people walking through the trees. There was no sign of a little black ghostly rabbit.

"Know what it is?" Neddie asked. We had stopped running and were standing bent over, our hands on our knees, breathing hard.

"No, what?" I asked.

"We're lost," Neddie said.

There was a low fence around the park, easy enough to climb over—and there we were, on a busy city street. Everything looked nearly normal. Nearly. There were people walking along, cars, buses, and taxicabs running, shops and apartment buildings. What was not quite normal was subtle. For example, doors are usually rectangular, but in this city, they never were—they were round, usually, sometimes oval. Same thing with windows—the ones in this city were not the window shapes we were used to seeing.

The clothes people had on were regular clothes, but just a little different from what you'd see on people in Los Angeles—not different colors, but different shades of colors. And there was something different about the light: it was just a tinge more orange than the light we had seen all our lives. When you're lost, ask a policeman—everybody knows that. Here came two of them, strolling along side by side.

"You kids look a little lost," one of the policemen said. "Anything we can do?"

The policemen had nice soft brown eyes and long, intelligent noses. Their fur was a rich golden-brownish color, and they had silky-looking floppy ears.

"The policemen are Labrador retrievers," Neddie whispered.

"Nonsense," Seamus whispered. "Labrador retrievers are about twenty-two inches at the shoulder. These policemen are much taller than that."

"Seriously, kids," the policeman said. "You look a little disoriented. Are you in any sort of trouble?"

Then one of the policemen whispered to the other, "Wait! That kid! Can it be? Is it him?" He was looking at Neddie.

Both policemen took out cards. The cards had a picture on them. They looked at the cards and they looked at Neddie. Then they looked at the cards again. "Is that him in the picture?"

"It isn't anyone else!"

"Yaaay for us! We got him!"

"Would you mind telling us your name?" one of the Labrador retriever policemen asked.

"It's Neddie," Neddie said.

"Well, I'll be an uncle's monkey," the policeman said.

"It is him! Neddie, we're going to have to ask you to come with us."

"Come with you?" Neddie asked. "Why?"

"We'll explain everything to you when we get downtown," the policeman said. Each of the policemen took Neddie by an elbow. "Just come along peacefully," they said.

"You're taking Neddie away?"

"We have to. We have his picture. We've been looking for him."

"But he didn't do anything. We just arrived here!"

"Of course he didn't. Of course you did."

"But what about us? Can we come along?"

"Sorry, kids. We don't have any instructions about you coming along."

"But we're lost!"

"If you're lost, ask a policeman—that is, ask another policeman. We have to take Neddie in now."

"At least tell us where we are."

"You are in New Yapyap City. Have a nice day."

CHAPTER 39

Neddie!

"Neddie! They took Neddie away!" I said.

"Took him *in*. They said they were taking him *in*," Seamus Finn said.

"We don't know where they took him," I said.

"They said they were taking him downtown," Seamus said.

"And we don't even know which way downtown is," I said.

"It's that way," someone said. We looked around. There was a girl, about our age, but taller and wider. She had long brown hair, nice eyes, and whiskers like a cat. "Was it Labrador retriever cops who took him?"

"They looked like Labrador retrievers," I said. "Are all the cops here Labrador retrievers?"

"Lots of them," the girl said. "They make good cops. They're polite and friendly, never give up, and they don't mind getting wet."

"Why did they arrest our friend, and where did they take him?" Seamus asked.

"Did he do anything?" the girl asked.

"We just got here," I said. "He didn't do anything. He didn't have time to do anything. The cops were already looking for him. They had a picture of him."

"Did they show you the picture?"

"No."

"Did they show your friend the picture?"

"I don't think so."

"They always have a picture. Labrador retrievers are very smart, but one picture of a human looks pretty much like another to them. They go more by scent."

"Oh."

"Where did you come from, some other plane of existence?" the girl with the cat whiskers asked.

"You know about that?" I asked.

"Oh, sure. Lots of tourists come here."

"Here being New Yapyap City?"

"Right. My name is Big Audrey," the girl said. "Probably your friend is at Juvenile Hole."

"Juvenile Hole? What is that?"

"It's where they take kids."

"Oh, I get it. Juvenile Hole is the street name for some official facility, probably Juvenile Hall, or Juvenile Holding, something like that," Seamus said.

"No, it's an actual hole," Big Audrey said. "They lower you into it."

"Then what happens?"

"Nothing bad, usually. They keep us for a couple of days and then let us out—most times. They ask us a lot of weird questions that don't make any sense, and then turn us loose, except in special cases."

"Why do they do that? Don't they like kids here?"

"Not much," Big Audrey said. "I didn't catch your names."

Seamus Finn and I introduced ourselves.

"So, I bet you're lost, don't have anyplace to stay, and don't know how to get home," Big Audrey said.

CHAPTER 40

Uncle Father Palabra

"**Y**ou may as well come home with me," Big Audrey said. "I see you're wearing rubber-soled shoes. That's good." We were both wearing basketball shoes.

"Why is it good?" I asked.

"Not afraid of heights, are you? Not scared of climbing something tall?" Big Audrey asked.

"Not me," I said. "I have been known to make my way along window ledges at the Hermione Hotel, which is eight stories high, and Seamus here is the son of the greatest swordsman in Hollywood, and an athlete in his own right."

"Good," Big Audrey said. "My uncle, Father Palabra, doesn't like people using the stairs or the elevator."

"Your uncle is your father?" Seamus Finn asked. "Or *a* father?"

"He's my uncle and he is a retired monk," Big Audrey said. "He is also a professor of mountaineering. You'll meet him in a few minutes. Follow me." We had been walking through the streets of New Yapyap City with Big Audrey.

Now she led us down a narrow space—it was too narrow to call it an alley—between two buildings. We had to turn sideways and squeeze between two brick walls just far enough apart to pass through. The space between the two walls got a bit wider all of a sudden—not a lot wider. There was a rope hanging down.

"What we have to do now is called chimneying," Big Audrey said. "What you do is take hold of the rope, brace your shoulders against the wall behind you, and place the soles of your feet against the opposite wall. Then you just walk up the wall, using your arms and the rope to help you, and keeping your shoulders firmly against the wall behind you. It's easy. Think you can do it?"

"Nothing to it," I said.

"Piece of cake," Seamus said.

"I'll go first," Big Audrey said. "We're going up twelve stories, so don't get confused and fall to your death, okay?"

Chimneying up twelve stories turned out not to be a piece of cake. Seamus admitted this. I admitted there was not nothing to it. But it was doable. We did it. It wasn't that it was physically so hard—it was more the idea that the higher we got the farther there was to fall. When we got to the top,

Big Audrey helped us onto a ledge. There was a sloping copper roof rising from the ledge.

"Now that the easy part is over, we need to rope up," Big Audrey said. She showed us how to loop the rope, which was waiting on the ledge, around us, and how to clip onto rings set in the sloping roof. "See, you clip onto this one, and then as you get past it, you clip onto the next one, unclip from the first one, and move that thing—it's called a carabiner—to the next ring beyond. This way, if you fall, it's only a few feet. When we get to the top of the roof, we will move along the ridge and then descend straight down when we come to the end. I'll show you how to do that when we get there."

Going straight down is called rappelling, and it is a little like chimneying, only you don't have anything to lean back against. We only had to rappel a few feet to get to Uncle Father Palabra's terrace, which was covered with pebbles and tufts of grass. There was a little penthouse, made of wood and looking like an Alpine cottage, and from the terrace there was a view of rooftops, looking like mountain peaks.

"You brought friends home, Audrey?" a voice called from inside the penthouse. "Anyone want pancakes?"

"I brought them the easy way, Uncle Father," Big

Audrey said. "They're from another plane of existence and not experienced climbers."

"That was the easy way?" I asked.

"Well the easiest way would be to come up in the elevator," Uncle Father Palabra said. "But that would be an insult to any able-bodied person."

"I wouldn't have been insulted," Seamus Finn said, rubbing his palms. We both had rope burns.

"Well, you are a polite and considerate young man," Uncle Father Palabra said. "What brings you to New Yapyap City from some other invisible world?" Uncle Father Palabra was short and strong-looking, and bald, with yellow eyes like a cat.

"All the ghosts in our . . . world . . . have been sneaking off to Old New Hackensack to attend some kind of witch's hootenanny or supernatural whoop-de-doo. We followed one and wound up here," I said.

"Their friend got picked up by a couple of Labradors," Big Audrey said. "He must be in Juvenile Hole."

"What did he do?" Uncle Father Palabra asked.

"Didn't do anything," Big Audrey said. "Didn't have time to do anything. They just now arrived through some rabbit hole."

"Well, everyone sit down and have some gooseberry

pancakes," Uncle Father Palabra said. "We'll see about getting your friend out of the Hole a little later."

"Why do they arrest kids here and put them in Juvenile Hole?" Seamus Finn asked.

"Just to be mean," Uncle Father Palabra said. "We don't like kids here in New Yapyap City—I don't mean me personally, but as a society."

The bottom floor of the penthouse was all one big room, and Uncle Father Palabra was in the kitchen area, making gooseberry pancakes. They smelled wonderful.

"Our schools are no good, kids aren't allowed to use the better parks, we feed them junky breakfast cereal that's full of sugar, sell their parents a lot of defective toys and expensive clothing, and give them stupid books to read, and stupid television programs, and throw them into Juvenile Hole for any reason at all, or no reason."

"You have television?" I asked. "We are just getting started with it in our world."

"I hope it's better than ours," Uncle Father Palabra said. "Ours would not keep a mouse's mind alive." I noticed an odd expression appear on Uncle Father Palabra's and Big Audrey's faces when Uncle Father Palabra said "mouse's," and thought about the fact that she had cat whiskers and he had cat eyes.

"You said we could see about getting Neddie out of

Juvenile Hole a little later," I said. "And these are wonderful pancakes."

"Yes, once it gets good and dark," Uncle Father Palabra said. "We might be able to do something."

CHAPTER 41

Something

While we ate our gooseberry pancakes and had cups of flowery tea, Uncle Father Palabra and Big Audrey asked us questions about where we came from, how we got here, and where we were going.

"If the ghostly bunny you were following is going to the supernatural wing-ding, she will have headed to New Old Hackensack," Uncle Father Palabra said. "That's the closest town to the Devil's Shoestring, a mountain with many interesting features. I've climbed it lots of times."

"Is New Old Hackensack far away?" I asked.

"Not very far," Big Audrey said. "But you have to cross the Mahakahakakatuk River to get there, and the Mahakahakakatuk is wide and scary, with things in it.

And there are many strange places with strange inhabitants between here and there."

"That's a heck of a name for a river," Seamus Finn said. "Is it an Indian name?"

"No, it is named for an explorer, Henry Mahakahakakatuk. The thing is, you will have to cross it in a coracle."

"What's a coracle?"

"Little round boat made of skin stretched over wooden branches. They're hard to steer and tippy. And you'll be crossing at night."

"Why a coracle? Aren't there any bigger boats that cross the river? And why at night?"

"A coracle because we have one, and you can't take a bigger boat, and it has to be at night because you will be fugitives from justice."

"Fugitives from justice? What did we do?"

"It's what you are going to do that will make you fugitives."

We heard voices and the sound of boots shuffling in the pebbles on the terrace. Two men with beards and pointy ears came in.

"These are our friends, the Farblonget brothers, Kevin and Kyle. Kevin and Kyle, meet Yggdrasil and Seamus. They are visitors from an alternate plane of existence, and their friend Neddie is a prisoner in Juvenile Hole," Uncle Father Palabra said.

"We ascended the east face of the Feeney Building," one of the Farblonget brothers said.

"Then we did a hand-traverse across the clock tower and leaped across to the roof of the Platt Building," said the other Farblonget brother.

"Then we belayed to the peak of the roof of this building, crawled along the ridgeline, and rappelled down to your terrace," the first Farblonget brother said.

"The brothers are studying mountaineering with Uncle Father," Big Audrey said. "It's urban mountaineering—we climb the buildings because we don't have any mountains."

"Very good work, boys," Uncle Father Palabra said. "Would you like some pancakes?"

I saw a head with curly golden hair appear at the edge of the terrace, and a woman with a small black nose and fuzzy cheeks and chin pulled herself up over the parapet.

"This is Gwendolyn Marshrat," Uncle Father Palabra said.

"I ascended the north face of your building, free-climbing all the way," Gwendolyn Marshrat said.

"Excellent," Uncle Father Palabra said. "Have some pancakes. A little later we are going to help a boy escape from Juvenile Hole."

"Mmmm! Do I smell gooseberries?" Gwendolyn Marshrat said.

CHAPTER 42

Why Exactly

"Why exactly did you come here?" Big Audrey asked us.

"Well, we heard about this big wing-ding or whoop-de-doo that was going to take place."

"On the Devil's Shoestring."

"Yes. All the ghosts were going. Ghosts love a good party. And since the ghosts weren't telling where they were going or how to get there, I decided I would find out." It was me telling this to Big Audrey.

"And you found out."

"In a way. In a way, I found out. This one ghost, a ghost of a bunny, named Chase, told me I ought to follow her."

"Which you did."

"Which we all did. And we wound up here. And now, I think it's very important for us to find Chase."

"So she can lead you to the big doings on the mountain."

"Well, now it's more so she can tell us how to get home. We have no idea."

"And since you know Chase was planning to head for the Devil's Shoestring . . ."

"That's where we'd better go too."

"This makes perfect sense to me," Big Audrey said. "After we get your friend Neddie out of Juvenile Hole, I will help you get started in the direction of New Old Hackensack, where we hope you will catch up with the ghostly bunny."

"That is very nice of you."

"I am a very nice person."

"Can we really get Neddie out of Juvenile Hole?"

"It so happens, you have run into the very people who can do it."

"Is it like a prison? Do they beat them and starve them? Have you ever been there?"

"I have been there. Mostly they try to persuade you to behave in an acceptable manner, and make you look at television so you will develop acceptable values. They make you look at a lot of commercials, so you will want to buy the things being advertised and become a useful member of society with a job to make money . . ."

"So you can buy the things in the advertisements."

"Yes."

"Does it work?"

"It works better on older kids and adults. In my opinion, this is why they don't like kids here. We don't fit into the commercial routine so well. New Yapyap City is all about commerce. What they say is that kids are messy and sloppy, leave food wrappers on the street, make noise, and play loud music. But that is just an excuse to treat us mean."

"So you think they throw kids in jail just 'cause they don't want to buy . . ."

"The latest shoes, clothing, music, movies, junky foods, things like that. Some kids fit in with no trouble, and some do after a few visits to the Hole. And some never do, and never will—that's me."

"Excuse my saying so, but it doesn't sound like a very nice place to be a kid."

"Not just New Yapyap City, but this whole region is ruled over by a tyrant. The city is the worst, though."

"A tyrant? What kind of tyrant? What's the tyrant's name?"

"Uncle."

"Uncle? Just Uncle?"

"We call him Uncle—not sure of the name—it may not even be the same uncle all the time. It could be the uncle, and his sons, or someone elects or appoints a new uncle every so often. I remember Uncle Rudy, Uncle Michael—there have even been female uncles."

"And they are called Aunt?"

"No, Uncle. It's like a title, like president, or mayor. Anyway, Uncle is strict and serious and not friendly to kids, all about keeping everything in perfect order, and protecting the people who own the most. They say he controls the police by witchcraft."

"I'd think you'd want to get out of town, especially if the tyranny and all that isn't as bad outside of town."

"Well, of course, I love Uncle Father, and being an urban mountaineer, and gooseberry pancakes, and there are nice things about the city too—but . . . you're right, it sort of stinks. Which is why I was thinking of going with you and your friends to find the ghostly rabbit and see the big supernatural party and everything . . . if that would be all right with you."

"We'd be delighted," Seamus Finn said.

CHAPTER 43

Shoofly Pie

While we waited for it to get dark enough to rescue Neddie, Uncle Father Palabra, the Farblonget brothers, Gwendolyn Marshrat, Big Audrey, Seamus Finn, and I ate gooseberry pancakes, drank cups of tea, and listened to Uncle Father Palabra tell stories of mountains and mountaineering. We also sang mountaineering songs—that is, everybody but Seamus Finn and I sang mountaineering songs. We didn't know any mountaineering songs. Seamus and I sang as much as we could remember of "When They Drop the Atomic Bomb." Everybody said it was a good song. Then we sang "Nature Boy." They liked that even better, and said it was like a mountaineering song.

It was cozy and friendly, sitting around eating pancakes

and drinking tea and telling stories and singing songs. The
Farblonget brothers and Gwendolyn Marshrat coiled lengths
of mountain-climbing rope and arranged pitons, carabiners,
ascenders, descenders, D-rings, and various other metal gim-
micks on loops of rope they attached to their belts. They also
had big rubber suction cups to be used when climbing on
windows and skylights.

"This is the plan," Uncle Father Palabra said. "Seamus
and Yggdrasil will take the elevator down to street level. I
know it is an inelegant way to descend, but you children are
inexperienced, and teaching you to travel from building to
building would take too much time. Audrey, you will go with
them, and the three of you will walk downtown. On your
way you will stop at Ogburn's Bakery and get a shoofly pie."

"A shoofly pie?"

"It's a kind of pie. Very good. And sticky," Uncle Father
Palabra said. "You will also go to our garage, which by good
luck is not far from Juvenile Hole, and get the coracle. Carry
that with you. It's quite light, and you shouldn't have any
trouble. Try to avoid meeting any police. The rest of us will
be waiting for you at the Hole."

"Then what happens?" I asked.

"Then we rescue your friend and you children take the
coracle down to the Mahakahakakatuk and set out. It's
quite straightforward."

"Yep," Big Audrey said.

"Nothing to it," I said.

"Piece of shoofly pie," Seamus Finn said.

CHAPTER 44

New Yapyap at Night

I have to say, New Yapyap City had some nice buildings. And the deserted streets at night were like deep canyons.

"It's even better from the rooftops," Big Audrey said. Ogburn's all-night bakery smelled wonderful. In addition to the shoofly pie, we got three large cookies to munch as we walked. They were chocolatey and salty, and still warm from the oven.

Big Audrey told us the names of some of the buildings as we passed them. They were all named for big companies. And there were a lot of stores with lighted display windows, lots of things for sale.

"This is Shin Bone Alley," Big Audrey said. "We have a garage here." We turned down a dark, narrow little street lined with low wooden buildings with wide doors. Audrey dug out a large key and opened the padlock on one of them. The inside was full of outdoor equipment, snowshoes and skis, coils of mountaineering rope, canvas bundles, ice axes, pots and pans, lanterns, and a big black thing that looked like some kind of enormous kitchen pot.

"The coracle," Big Audrey said. "It's light. I can carry it myself. You guys take these paddles." Seamus and I took hold of four canoe paddles, and Big Audrey lifted the coracle over her head like a huge umbrella. "Next stop is the Hole," she said.

CHAPTER 45

The Hole

Juvenile Hole was perfectly round, with straight sides, like a well. It was maybe thirty or forty feet deep. There were benches in the bottom, with maybe a dozen kids sitting, looking at a big TV screen. There were no cops or guards, just what looked like a TV camera that ran around the inside of the bottom of the hole on tracks, the lens pointed in at the kids on the benches. Some of the kids had ratty-looking blankets over their shoulders. We tried to pick out which one was Neddie.

As we peered into the Hole, we became aware of Uncle Father Palabra, the Farblonget brothers, and Gwendolyn Marshrat beside us.

"Which one is your friend?" Uncle Father Palabra whispered.

"He's there, sitting at the end," Seamus whispered back.

"Let's do this," Uncle Father Palabra said. Uncle Father Palabra and one of the Farblonget brothers stood at the edge of the hole and lowered Gwendolyn Marshrat and the other Farblonget brother. Gwendolyn had the shoofly pie with her. She slapped the shoofly pie over the lens of the TV camera on tracks. It stuck. Then the two of them scooped Neddie up, under the arms, and Uncle Father Palabra and the other Farblonget brother reeled them up. It didn't take more than fifteen seconds.

"Say, there's a place here in town where you can get a hamburger that weighs three-quarters of a pound," Neddie said. "It has special sauce, and it is made with Japanese kobe-style beef, whatever that is, and it's a limited-time offer. Can we stop and get one?"

"Brainwashing works," Big Audrey said.

"Get going," Uncle Father Palabra said. We four kids made for the Mahakahakakatuk, with Audrey and Seamus holding the coracle over us, and all of us underneath it, our scampering feet sticking out below. We must have looked like a big black turtle scooting along the sidewalk.

"This reminds me of something," Neddie said.

From behind us we heard a voice blaring over a loudspeaker: "Who put a shoofly pie over the lens of the television camera?"

And we heard Uncle Father Palabra shout, "It was I, Norman! Norman put the shoofly pie on your fershlugginer lens!"

"Hee hee!" Big Audrey giggled. "Now they're going to think Norman did it."

The next thing I knew, we were in the coracle on the river, the big Mahakahakakatuk, paddling and spinning.

CHAPTER 46

Big River

"This is Big Audrey," I told Neddie. "She and a bunch of other people rescued you from Juvenile Hole."

"Pleased to meet you, and thanks very much," Neddie said. "They have the biggest television screen I've ever seen down there. We have better programs in Los Angeles, but they have better ads in New Yapyap City. What kind of boat is this?"

"It's a coracle," Big Audrey said.

"It's round."

"It's all we've got. My uncle, Uncle Father Palabra, built it. Ancient type of boat."

"It doesn't steer all that well," Neddie said. That was the truth. The coracle had a tendency to spin and it careened all over the river. After a while, we started to get the hang of it. With two people paddling and two others using their paddles as rudders at the front and the back of the boat—assuming it had a front and a back—we could get it to go more or less in one direction.

"What river is this?" Neddie wanted to know.

"It's the Mahakahakakatuk," Big Audrey said. "The object is to get to the other side."

"How long would it take if we were in something normal?" I asked.

"I don't know. Maybe half an hour."

"And as we are?"

"It looks like it will take all night—hours, anyway."

"What are those hissing and clicking noises?"

"There are things in the river."

"Bad things?"

"Well, I wouldn't dangle my fingers in the water," Big Audrey said.

"Have you been on the river before?" I asked.

"No. People don't go on the river much. It's the things. This is the first time the coracle has been in the water, too. Considering Uncle Father built it from pictures in an encyclopedia, it's working fairly well, I'd say."

"It feels like something is gnawing on my oar," I said.

"I wouldn't be surprised," Big Audrey said. "What exactly are the things in this river?" Seamus Finn asked.

"Mostly eel-sharks," Big Audrey said.

"And they're bad?"

"How good can something that's an eel and a shark be?" There was an evil-smelling mist rising from the river, and the moon lit up patches of greasy-looking slime. We were quiet and serious as we paddled and steered for the far shore and listened to the hissing and clicking.

"At least there aren't any whales in this river," Seamus Finn said after a long time.

"Oh, there are," Big Audrey said. "They eat the eel-sharks."

We kept steering and paddling.

CHAPTER 47

Kind Hearts and Crunchy Granola

Dawn broke on the river. We were getting close to the shore. We were tired and hungry, and our hands were sore.

"Travel by *coracle* is the worst," Neddie said. "Who invented them, anyway?"

"Well, the word *coracle* comes from the Welsh *cwrwgl*," Big Audrey said. "But they go back thousands of years, and similar boats turn up in all kinds of cultures. The *curragh* is an Irish boat, the Mandan Indians made bull boats, and the Iraqi *gufa*, the southern Indian *parisal*, and the Tibetan *ku-dru* are all along the same lines. As you can see, it's basically a big basket with hide stretched over it and tar spread over that to make it waterproof. And you have to admit, it got us where we wanted to go."

"Do you have Wales, and Mandan Indians, and Tibet in this world, same as ours?" Neddie asked.

"Apparently," Big Audrey said.

"I want to go someplace where they're serving breakfast," I said.

"Look!" Seamus Finn said. "People!"

"Or Munchkins," I said.

There were people! Short people! They were up to their middles, which would be up to our knees, in the river, scooping up fish in nets. They were all at least eighty years old and had long white hair—the men had long beards. They were wearing clothes in all the colors of the rainbow, and some of them had headbands—also rainbow-colored—flowers in their hair, and bead necklaces and bracelets. We paddled closer.

"Dude!" one of the old people said. "It's kids in a coracle!"

"Far out!" another old person said.

"Heavy!" said another one.

"Aren't you afraid of the eel-sharks, standing in the water like that?" Seamus asked the old people.

"No hassle, man," one of the old bearded guys said. "They know we're cool. We do our thing and they do theirs. I bet you kiddies would like some breakfast. Help us carry the baskets of fish and we'll lay some nutrition on you."

We beached the coracle and helped the weird old people carry baskets of fish up the bank.

"What do you do with the fish?" I asked them.

"We smoke them."

"Oh, and then you sell them?"

"Huh?"

The old folks lived in a collection of tents, shacks, and broken-down school buses. Everything was painted in every color, just like their clothing. Introductions were made. They had names like Sunflower, Safflower, Cornflower, Wholewheatflower, Sun, Moon, Star, Sunshine, Moonshine, Weirdbeard, Popdaddy, and Woovy Groovy.

Breakfast was something Gypsy Boots would have been proud of—fruit, juice, cereal consisting of oats, almonds, prunes, and raisins, and French toast made with health bread with nuts and seeds and twigs and things in it. The old people were friendly. They told us they were hoopies, which meant they had dropped out of society, lived peacefully, and didn't harm any living thing, except fish. They said they tried to live in such a way that they would not be hassled by Uncle. They called him The Man. They also felt strongly that, if possible, one should try never to piss off a witch. Mama Banana seemed to be the head hoopie. She asked us lots of questions about where we had come from and where we were going.

"So you're going to make the scene at the annual super-natural freak-out on the Devil's Shoestring? It's a hassle getting there, but you should do your own thing. I mean, we create our own reality. You children are welcome to crash here for as long as you like." Then all the hoopies got out guitars, and whistles, and drums and bells, and spent the rest of the morning making music.

We stayed with the hoopies for a while. They were easy to be around, and we liked the healthy food and the music. We helped them fish, when they felt like fishing, and spent time wandering in the woods above the river, collecting flowers and mushrooms, all of which we ate or wore. And Sunbeam, Moonbeam, and Rainbeam showed us how to dye our clothes all colors, like theirs.

When we decided it was time to do our own thing and split, the sweet old hoopies gave us love beads and told us to create our own reality, and be mindful of karma. Karma is what happens to you because of what you did—every action has a reaction, and if you live groovily, you will have groovy experiences.

We knew the general direction we needed to go. The hoopies had never been as far as the Devil's Shoestring, because going so far was just such a drag, man. We started up the path, carrying bags of granola, with flowers in our hair. The hoopies cried and waved goodbye.

"Stay on the road! Don't play cards with strangers! If you meet a witch, don't piss her off! Don't piss off a witch! Don't trust anyone over ninety!" they called after us.

CHAPTER 48

My Name

In addition to the granola and flowers, Mama Banana had given me another gift. She told me about my name. "Do you know what your name means, little one?" Mama Banana, the matriarch of the hoopies, asked me. Calling me "little one" struck me as a little funny, since Mama Banana was well under four feet tall.

"I was always told it meant 'Odin's Steed,'" I said. "Odin being one of the Norse gods. 'Ygg' means 'terrible,' one of Odin's nicknames, and 'drasil' means 'horse' or 'steed.' So Odin's Steed, or the Terrible One's Horse."

"Did no one ever tell you about another meaning of the name? Have you ever heard of Yggdrasil the World Tree?"

"Oh, yes," I said. "There was something about a tree, but I never got that part straight."

"Well, the old Norse folks made some weird connection between trees and horses, for some reason—so they might give a tree a name like the Terrible One's Horse, and it's a tree, always was a tree, was never anything but a tree, and there isn't an actual horse in the story. Don't ask me why."

"Not rational, huh?"

"And a long time ago. Parts of the puzzle are missing. Anyway, Yggdrasil, also called the World Tree, is a giant ash tree that links together all the various worlds."

"So the ancient Norse knew there were different worlds, or planes of existence?"

"Yep. And the thing that connects them is the tree: Yggdrasil."

"Cool. So it is kind of neat that I come from a different world, and here I am in this one."

"It is neat. Beneath the three roots of the tree are the realms of Asgard, Jotunheim, and Niflheim. There are three wells, too: Mimisbrunnr, which is guarded by Mimir; Urdarbrunnr, which is guarded by the Norns; and Hvergelmir, the source of many rivers."

"Who and what are all those?"

"No idea, but it sounds cool, doesn't it? Four deer run across the branches of the tree and eat the buds—there's a squirrel named Ratatosk who carries gossip, and Vidofnir, a rooster who perches at the very top. There's a snake called Nidhogg who gnaws on the roots, and on the day of Ragnarok—that's when the whole universe is destroyed, but don't worry, it starts over again—a giant named Surt will set the whole thing on fire."

"Some tree. I have to get a book and read about all this stuff."

"We used to have a book. It was about a little girl piglet who lived in an apartment."

"So my name is the name of the tree that connects the different worlds."

"Nine of them."

"My last name is Birnbaum. Does that mean anything?"

"Yep. Pear tree."

"A tree again!"

"You're a tree person."

"I like it. Thanks, Mama Banana."

"Oh! I just remembered who the Norns are. They are like the fates, also like witches, but not exactly. By the way, try not to get a witch pissed off at you. Anyway, some stories say that every person has a Norn who takes care of him or her."

I hoped I had a Norn, and it was about Yggdrasil the World Tree, and the old Norse myths, and how I was a tree person that I was thinking as we walked along.

CHAPTER 49

On the Road

"So we just continue along this little road," Big Audrey said. "And eventually it will take us to New Old Hackensack. Nothing to it."

"And we should keep a lookout for a ghostly black bunny on the way," I said.

"So, how long will it take us to get to New Old Hackensack?" Neddie Wentworthstein asked.

"The hoopies didn't say. They seemed to think it was too far for them, but they're really old. Probably isn't that far, really."

It was a winding dirt road, just wide enough for a single car—only there were no cars. There were no houses either, just woods and fields. The weather was mild, the sky was blue, a little breeze was blowing, there were flowers blooming along the roadside. It was a perfect day for walking. Now and then we would come to a cold, clear stream and drink the best-tasting water. When we got hungry, we dipped into the bags of crunchy granola and fresh fruit the hoopies had given us.

"So, what do we do when night comes? Just sleep on the ground next to the road?" Neddie asked.

"I guess so," Big Audrey said. "Unless we find some kind of shelter."

"I hope it doesn't rain," Seamus Finn said.

"It doesn't look like rain," I said.

"You'd think there would be a house, or a person, or a sign or something," Neddie said.

"It doesn't look like wild forest," Big Audrey said. "I mean, this is a road, not just a path—someone must use it—and some of the fields are cultivated, so there must be farmers who take care of them."

"Yes, but where are they?" Neddie said.

"It's getting late," I said. "The sun is getting low."

"It will be dark before long," Seamus said.

"Getting a little cooler, too," Big Audrey said.

"Yes."

"Yes."

CHAPTER 50

Gingerbread House

We walked. The sun was setting. Lower and lower. Shadows got longer. Then the rim of the sun disappeared behind distant hills. The sky got purple. The breeze was starting to feel a bit chilly. Nobody said anything. The twilight was deepening.

And then.

"A light!" Neddie said.

"Yes! A light!"

It was a friendly yellow light, twinkling through the trees. As we rounded a curve, we could see it plainly. Not far off. It was a house!

"Should we go there?" Seamus asked.

"Yes!" we all said.

"Maybe there's a barn or something we could sleep in," I said.

"Maybe there are hoopies, or other nice people there," Big Audrey said.

We were running across the fields. As we got closer, we could make out the house more clearly in the fading light. It was a nice house. It was sweet. It had pointy roofs, and three porches, and several chimneys. It was painted in many colors, and there were all kinds of carving and scroll-work, spindles, cutouts, little spidery bits of woodwork.

"What a fancy house!" Big Audrey said. "What kind of house do you call this?"

I knew. "It's a Victorian house. All the decoration was popular in the nineteenth century. It's called gingerbread. This is what you call a gingerbread house." The friendly yellow light was a porch light. The windows were lit up too, with a warm glow. There were flower beds bordering a winding gravel path that led to the gingerbread house. And we could smell a wonderful smell—someone was baking something. It made our mouths water.

We stopped just short of the porch with the light and stood in a little knot, deciding what we should do and say. "We can just say we are travelers and ask if there is a barn we can sleep in."

"Maybe we should just ask if we can have a glass of

water and wait and see if they are friendly and invite us in."

"We could offer to do some kind of work around the place in return for shelter for the night and maybe something to eat."

"What if we just knock on the door and then stand there looking cute?"

"Or pathetic! Pathetic might be good."

"How about cute *and* pathetic?"

"Yes! We'll do that!"

Before we could set foot on the porch, the door opened. There was a tall, thin woman, sort of old, but not old like the hoopies. She had gray hair done up tightly, in a neat bun, and a long gray dress.

"Why, it's children!" the woman said. "And what nice-looking children! Where can you have come from? Come closer, into the light, so I can see you. Oh! Such lovely children! Come in! Come in, children! I have hot apple pie! And milk! Come in! Come in!"

We crowded into the nicest, neatest, sweetest, friendliest, prettiest old kitchen any of us had ever seen. The smell of hot apple pie was so thick, we could almost see it. There were old-fashioned carved chairs, and a kitchen table to match. The stove was old-fashioned, black and made of iron. There were four or five fat, contented-looking pussycats curled up on cushions near the stove, purring and licking their paws.

"Sit down, children! Sit down. You must tell me who you are and what you are doing way out here in the country at night. I have cold milk, and the pies are just cooled enough to eat. Isn't it lucky I baked pies? Come, children, sit. My name is Wanda. I hope none of you is afraid of pussycats. I have many pussycats, more than just these. I have, oh, millions of cats. Now who wants a slice of cheddar cheese on their pie?"

Millions of Cats

While we sat in Wanda's cozy kitchen eating apple pie with cheddar cheese, various cats walked in and out. She didn't have millions of them, but she had a lot. Every time a cat turned up, she would talk to it, tell us its name, and say something like, "Look, Sweetums! We have lovely children visiting us!" I guessed Wanda was a sweet old crazy woman who lived alone and had just the cats for company. The pie was fantastic.

We told Wanda about crossing the river in a coracle and visiting the hoopies. We didn't mention that we had busted Neddie out of Juvenile Hole in New Yapyap City. That might have made us sound like desperate characters. And we told her we were going to New Old Hackensack.

"So you walked all day, poor dears," Wanda said. "You must be tired and footsore. I have lovely beds, all made up. Come, I will show you where to sleep, and in the morning, perhaps you would like to help me feed the cats?" We told Wanda we would be happy to help her feed the cats.

"Are you sure? You know, I have a great many cats." We told her we would be happy to help feed the cats, no matter how many there were.

"You are such wonderful, polite, helpful children," Wanda said. "And you will help me until all the cats are fed?"

"Of course."

"And you won't go until all the cats have been cared for?"

"Certainly. We will stay until every cat has been cared for. It's the least we can do after your kindness."

"Such superior children. I wish you were mine and I could keep you always. Come, and let me show you to your beds."

Upstairs in Wanda's house there was a large room, warm and dry. In each corner was a little bed with a thick, fluffy quilt. Just looking at the beds made us realize how tired we were after our long walk. We crawled under the quilts, snuggled down, and were asleep in a minute. And it felt like a minute later when we heard Wanda saying,

"Time to get up, children! Wake up, wake up! There are pussycats to care for!"

We sat up in our beds, rubbing our eyes. It was still dark outside.

"Hurry, children! Hurry and wash! Line up and take your turn! The pussycats are waiting!" When I was splashing cold water on my face, trying to wake up, I noticed something in the washstand mirror. There was a little green collar around my neck. It had a little bell on it. I turned it around and around, trying to find where it fastened, but it was all one piece. When I came out of the bathroom, I saw that the other kids had collars, too: Neddie's was red, Seamus's was blue, and Big Audrey's was yellow, all with little bells.

"What are these?"

"No idea. How'd they get there?"

"I can't get mine off."

"Me neither."

"Come, children! Help Wanda stir up the big bowls of food for the pussycats!"

Wanda gave each of us a large metal bowl full of disgusting goo, and a big wooden spoon.

"Now mix up the disgusting goo and start spooning it into the little pussycat bowls. Hurry, children—we have millions of cats to feed."

Again, there were not millions of cats. There were only a thousand, or maybe two thousand. They were hungry, switching their tails and mewing, rubbing against our legs, and batting us with their paws.

"Faster, children, faster! We have to feed all the cats before we start scooping out the litter boxes!"

"Scooping out the litter boxes?"

"Oh, yes! And then we have to wash all the bowls, and dry them. Then we have to brush the kitties and look for hairballs. So much to do! I am lucky to have you children to help me."

CHAPTER 52

All Day Long

It was ladle out goo, scoop out litter boxes, wash bowls, brush kitties, and scrape up hairballs at a rapid rate. Wanda kept encouraging us and telling us to work faster—and we worked fast. We worked faster than we wanted to. We couldn't slow down for some reason. I noticed a couple of things: all of Wanda's cats had the same kind of little collars, with bells, that we kids were wearing—and every time I thought of taking a break, the bell on my collar would jingle and Wanda would appear before me, urging me to work faster.

While Big Audrey and I were washing pussycat bowls, I whispered to her, "Am I mistaken, or is Wanda a witch?"

"I don't see how she could be anything else," Big Audrey whispered back.

"Why don't we all just burst out the door and run like the dickens?" I whispered.

Both our bells jingled, and Wanda was suddenly there. "Thinking of running away? Oh, no, no, no—that would never do. There is too much work left, and besides, Wanda is baking pies! Nice pies! Keep working, dear children!" It was night and we had fed all the cats, twice, scooped ever so many litter boxes, washed and washed and washed bowls, and we were so tired we could barely drag our feet to the table.

"It's apple pie again, dear children!" Wanda said. "Eat all you want! Then sleep. So much to do tomorrow." Wanda wandered off to mix up vats of goo to feed the cats in the morning. We were left sitting slumped in our chairs, barely able to lift a fork.

"She's a witch, you know," Seamus whispered.

"Yes. We figured that out."

"We're captives here," Neddie said.

"Knew that too."

"She's going to work us to death," Neddie said.

"Nope, she's not," Seamus said.

"How do you know?" I asked.

"Look around. Look at everybody. See anything different?"

First, I looked at Big Audrey. Except for looking like someone who had tended thousands of cats all day, she looked pretty much as usual: pretty girl, large, nice eyes, and whiskers like a cat—same as always. Only maybe she looked a little more catlike than I remembered.

Then I looked at Neddie. He had cat whiskers too!

And Seamus had them!

"Yep. You've got 'em too," Seamus said. "I expect all the cats here were kids, or people, once. She's going to work us until we all turn into pussycats."

"What? Do you mean these whiskers are the first change, and we'll all be pussycats in the end?"

"That's my theory."

"How do you know it isn't just puberty setting in?"

"If you think that, I can guess what grade you got in your health class. No, we are on the way to pussycat-hood, unless we figure out some way to escape."

All our collar bells jingled, and Wanda appeared. "No escape! No escape, dear little children. Now off to bed with you. You don't want Wanda getting pissed off at you."

"No, ma'am, don't want that," we all said, and climbed the stairs to our beds. "Don't want to get a witch pissed off at us."

I was too tired not to fall asleep immediately, though I knew I really ought to lie awake and worry. Sometime in the middle of the night, I felt a hand across my mouth. It was Neddie's.

"Don't make a sound, and try not to think," he whispered. "Seamus had an idea, and we're trying it out." I felt Neddie feel around for the little bell on my collar and whack it with a small hard object.

"It's my turtle," he whispered. "It's supposed to be some kind of magic. Seamus suggested I smack the bells with it. They're pretty chintzy and easy to smash. With the bells out of commission, maybe we can . . . you know."

"You mean . . ."

"Don't say it! Don't think it. Just be ready when Wanda is busy mixing up goo."

CHAPTER 53

Like a Charm

"I'm thinking about escaping," Seamus said in a low voice, not to be heard over the ruckus the hungry cats were making. His squashed bell did not jingle, and neither did any of ours.

"Neat! Works like a charm," Neddie said. "Let's streak out the door!"

"Nothing is stopping us except that big iron padlock," Big Audrey said.

We hadn't noticed before. There was a big, rusty, heavy old-fashioned padlock fastening the door on the inside.

"We'll be needing the key," Seamus said.

"Obviously."

"Of course, Wanda has it," I said.

Wanda was off in the kitchen, mixing up the goo. We could hear her talking to the cats. She would be hollering for us to start dishing it out in a minute. "I think she wears it on her belt," Neddie said.

"We'll have to filch it," Seamus said.

"Is any one of us good at filching?" I asked.

"I can filch," Seamus said. "All I need is someone to distract her."

"I should warn you that filching things from a witch may tend to piss her off," Big Audrey said. "And I speak from experience."

"I was wondering why you already had cat's whiskers," I said. "Previous encounter with a witch?"

"I'll tell you about it another time," Big Audrey said. "Now, the traditional thing would be to stuff her into her own oven. Who's for that?"

"Why try to improve on a classic?" Seamus said. "We shove her into the oven, and as she goes in, I filch the key. Now, do we shove her into a cold oven, or wait until it's cooking?"

"Euwww!"

"It's in the stories," Seamus said. "But I assume we are going with the cold oven."

"Yes!"

It turned out to be a relative cinch. We were in the

kitchen, getting more goo, and Wanda was in the next room, spooning.

"Wanda! Wanda!" we shouted. "There's a pussycat way back in the oven and we can't get it to come out!" Wanda bustled into the kitchen and stuck her head into the oven.

"Come out, little pussycat!" she said. We all put our backs against her wide rump and pushed as hard as we could. At the same moment, Seamus filched the key off her belt. Then we slammed the oven door.

"I can't believe I fell for that old trick!" Wanda shrieked. "Wanda is really pissed off!"

"Unlock the door! Unlock the door!" we shouted to one another, and were outside and running across the fields in the next second. Behind us we could hear Wanda shrieking, and a thousand cats mewing . . . and cheering . . . cheering in the voices of children.

"I think the pussycats are changing back into kids," I said.

"This is good. Wanda will be chasing them every which way, once she manages to get out of the oven," Seamus said.

"But the ones she really wants to catch will be us," Big Audrey said. "We should get as far away as we can, as fast as we can."

"Then it would be good if we flagged down that car and begged for a ride," Neddie said.

"Car?"

There was a car coming down the road, a big car with big wheels, going fairly fast and making clouds of dust, the horn honking constantly. We spread out across the road, jumped up and down, and waved our arms frantically. The car, which was bright red, with a lot of shiny brass work, screeched to a stop.

At the wheel was a tiny, extremely ugly, and splotchy driver, wearing goggles, a thick muffler around his neck, a flat cap, a big overcoat, and big gloves. "Give us a ride! Give us a ride, please!" we shouted.

The little driver leaned over and opened the door.

"Where to, kiddies?" he asked in a croaky voice.

"Old New Hackensack . . . or anywhere! Please! Please!"

"Hop in."

We all piled in. Then he jammed the car into gear and took off so fast, we were thrown against the seatbacks. In ten minutes we were at least ten miles away from Wanda's house, with no sign of slowing down. The little driver threw the car into the curves and ground the gears. The tires squealed, and he beeped the horn every few seconds for no apparent reason.

"At this rate we'll be well clear of her in no time," I said.

"Look! We still have the whiskers," Seamus said.

"Actually, I sort of like them," I said.

"Everyone does," Big Audrey said.

CHAPTER 54

Back on the Road

Except for comments like "How do you like my car?" "Isn't she a beauty?" "I just bought her yesterday," and "Beep beep!" the little driver didn't talk much. He spoke only one other word while driving the car. That word was "Drat!"

He said it when he drove the car into a large tree that was actually nowhere near the road. We were shaken up, but no one was hurt.

"End of the road! Beep beep! Cheerio!" the little driver said. Then he just hopped out of the car and took off in a series of very long, slow leaps, across the fields and out of sight.

"Everybody okay?" I asked.

"Yes—he hit the tree fairly softly," Big Audrey said.

"Was that guy a frog or toad of some kind?" Seamus asked.

"Whatever he was, he came along at the right time," Neddie said. "We're miles and miles away from Wanda's, and we must be getting close to New Old Hackensack."

"Well, let's pull ourselves together and get back on the road," Big Audrey said.

We hadn't gone very far when something happened that none of us could explain. We ran into a tree! We just, all four of us, collided with it, the same way the froggy little driver had crashed the car! *Smack!* We all bumped into it at the same time, and found ourselves sitting on the ground.

"How is this possible?" we asked each other. "How could we just walk into a tree?"

Then it started to rain on us. When I say on us, I mean just on us. It was bright sunshine to the left and the right, behind us and before us, and there was a small black rain cloud over our heads, drenching us. When we moved, the cloud moved with us. We tried running, and the cloud speeded up. We were getting drenched. When we bumped into another tree, we huddled under the branches, trying to shelter from the rain.

"What's going on?" I asked. "We're walking into trees,

it's raining on us and nowhere else—it's almost as if . . ."

"Seems pretty obvious," a voice that didn't belong to any of us said. "Looks to me as though you kids have managed to piss off a witch."

There was a tall hooded figure standing just outside our circle of rain.

"Where did you come from?" we asked, surprised.

"Same as you: L.A. in its appropriate world. I'm on my way to the big supernatural whoop-de-doo on the Devil's Shoestring."

"Wait a second!" Neddie said. "I know that voice! Melvin?"

Melvin the shaman pulled back his hood and smiled broadly at us. "Hello, wet kids," he said.

"You know this geek?" Big Audrey asked.

"Yes, he's a shaman," I said.

"Can you tell us how to get out from under this rain cloud?"

"Did you piss off a witch?"

"It was unavoidable. She was turning us into pussycats."

"I noticed the whiskers. I sort of like them."

"Everyone does. How about it? Can you get us out of this?"

"Well, of course I could," Melvin the shaman said. "But, you know, a journey like the one you're taking—

it's sort of a personal quest. You encounter adversity, you suffer, you overcome, you gain deep knowledge of yourselves. It's spiritual. If I were to show you some cheap trick to get you out of being as wet as a bunch of drowned rats, it might diminish the experience in some way. Would you want that?"

"Yes!" we all shouted.

"You're sure you wouldn't rather figure it out for yourselves?"

"No!"

"Okay, do you want me to show you how to stop the rain only, or reverse the whole curse?"

"Reverse the curse! Reverse the curse!"

"You realize by accepting this easy expedient you're taking all the depth out of the whole story."

"We don't care! We don't care!"

"It won't be meaningful or revelatory."

"We're soaking! We're drowning! Get on with it!"

"All right. Turn your pockets inside out and dance around like idiots."

"What?"

"Just do it."

We turned out our pockets and danced around like idiots, as best we could. The little rain cloud instantly vanished.

"That was all there was to it?" we asked Melvin.

"Sure, it looks easy once someone tells you how," he said. "I'm a little sorry I interrupted your authentic experience. On the other hand, I happen to know that next she was going to have you attacked by volcanos, so maybe it was for the best."

"Are you going to walk to Old New Hackensack? May we come with you?"

"I walk incredibly fast. You couldn't keep up. Besides, if we all traveled together, it would be my journey with you tagging along, instead of your journey. Also, you're all soaking wet and smell of apple pie and kitty litter. I'll see you at the festival." Melvin the shaman strode off. Then he stopped, turned around, and said, "By the way, the road will take you through the Valley of the Shlerm, or Shlermental. You may find it interesting. Don't stay too long and miss the doings at the Devil's Shoestring."

Then, he took another stride, picked up speed, and was actually making a cloud of dust by the time he disappeared in the distance.

"That guy is some fast walker," Big Audrey said.

"Professional shaman," Neddie said. "Taught me all I know."

CHAPTER 55

Walking Along

As we walked along, we sang. We sang "The Cry of the Wild Goose," about a guy whose heart must go where the wild goose goes, and he turns into a goose, leaving just a few feathers behind for his wife to try to figure out.

The sun dried us as we walked along, and inspired by Melvin's fast walking, we kept up a good pace. Swinging our arms, we walked four abreast along the road, singing songs as the miles went by. Besides "The Cry of the Wild Goose," we sang "Mule Train," and the song from the movie *High Noon*. All good walking songs.

"What is that, a church steeple?" Neddie asked, pointing to something in the distance. It didn't look exactly like a steeple. As we got closer, we saw it clearer, rising above the trees.

"It's a tower of some kind. Made of stone." Then as we got closer still, we saw another tower, and then another.

"Look! It's a whole castle!"

The road had been going gradually upward for a long time, not steep enough to make walking harder, but always taking us higher. Now we came to the crest and found we were looking down into a green valley. The castle was on the slopes of the opposite side of the valley, and it was a fancy one—it looked like an illustration in some old children's book. Below the castle were little houses, cultivated fields, and a thick forest.

"It must be the Valley of the Shlerm!" Seamus said.

"Also known as the Shlermental," Neddie said.

"It looks like the Middle Ages or something," I said.

"Look! The houses have thatched roofs, and there are carts pulled by some kind of animals," Big Audrey said.

"What are they, oxen?" Seamus asked.

"No. Oxen have horns and are sort of like cows," I said. "These look more like extremely large . . ."

"Skunks!" Big Audrey said.

We stuck our noses into the air and sniffed.

"Yep. Skunks."

"Skunks?"

"Skunks. Woodpussies, polecats, zorillos, mephitidae, stinkbadgers, Pepé Le Pews, funksquirters."

"I never knew they got so big."

"Well, it's a sweet little valley—in certain respects."

"Shall we go down?"

"Why not? A smell can't kill you."

"Let's hope."

CHAPTER 56

The Valley of the Shlerm

It wasn't that bad. It wasn't as though a skunk had lost its temper and let fly in the vicinity. There was just that slight tinge of skunkiness that hangs in the air when a skunk is around—in this case, a lot of skunks, and enormous ones. We were getting used to it.

"Come, children, gather round. I have grapes and cheese, and fresh spring water. Come, and listen to the old stories, and partake." It was an old guy sitting on a rock by the side of the road. He was wearing a beat-up straw hat, and a kind of smock that came down to his knees. He had cloth leggings crisscrossed with rope, and on his feet there were rags that looked to be stuffed with straw.

"Come, children, don't be shy. You are footsore and

hungry travelers. Come and refresh yourselves." The old guy spread a clean cloth on the ground and out of a big leathern bag took cheese, bunches of purple grapes, a round loaf of bread that was crusty on the outside and chewy on the inside, and a stoneware bottle full of ice-cold spring water. The cheese was great, not like any cheese I had ever tasted, and it went perfectly with the grapes. We took long swigs from the stone bottle while the old guy looked on, beaming.

"I am Grivnek," he said. We told him our names. "Eat, children, eat and drink all you want."

When we had eaten and drunk all we wanted, Grivnek closed his eyes and began to speak.

"In the days before Uncle came, there was a king in the Shlermental. In those days our people were prosperous and happy. Our maidens were the fairest, with arms like bolognas and legs like bottles of beer. Our swains all had golden hair and were tall and stupid.

"And heroes! We had heroes! In those days, our brave men were not afraid to venture into the dark forest of Shlerm, the dark forest where the ravens live. They were not afraid to visit the quivering bog.

"Nafnek was the name of our king, and he was wise and just. The people were happy and content. They tended their garlic fields, raised beautiful skunks, danced and sang. But Nafnek came to die and was succeeded by his son, Foofnik, who was foolish and cruel. He taxed and punished the people, played Ping-Pong on the Sabbath, and mocked our ancient customs. The people were unhappy, and hated Foofnik.

"Then Uncle came, a stranger from far away. He spoke of throwing off the yoke of Foofnik's cruelty. He spoke of democracy, and the people rose up against Foofnik and drove him away. Then, for a time, happiness returned to the Shlermental. The people governed themselves, we sent our garlic to Old New Hackensack and New Yapyap City, and received gold, with which we bought Hershey bars, and nice shoes, and other fine things.

"Uncle led us, and also led the great cities, and all the country around. His administration was fair and efficient. The roads were maintained, the drinking water was clean, the price of garlic was controlled, children were taught to read and write, and there was ice cream in the summer.

"Then there was a catastrophe. A huge storm struck us. Trees were uprooted, houses fell down, and fields were under water. The garlic crop was lost, the skunks ran wild in the forest, and the roads could not be traveled. The people of the Shlermental were in despair. What could be done? All seemed lost. But Uncle came to our rescue, or so he thought. From somewhere he found helpers, a group of powerful people who were skilled in magic. By magical means they repaired the damage and restored everything to the way it had been.

"These people were witches, and not nice ones. They were bad witches. After they had completed their work, they stayed. They stayed with Uncle as his council of helpers. Uncle thought they were helping him, but really they had taken the power. Instead of a democracy, we had a witchocracy. Conditions are not as bad as in Foofnik's day, but we are not free."

"Wow, that is some story," we said. "What are you— a wise man, a storyteller, the village elder?"

"No. None of those things. I am the village idiot."

CHAPTER 57

We Discover More

"Well, my lunch break is over," Grivnek said. "Back to work now."

He stuffed the picnic cloth back into his leathern bag and went off, wandering from one side of the road to the other, saying things like "Hoo! Haa! Humma humma! Goo! Arr! Bibble bibble. Hee hee hee," and picking up twigs and leaves and tossing them into the air over his head.

"Nice fellow," Neddie said.

"And a very competent idiot," Seamus said. "See how he walks normally for a couple of steps, and then shuffles. That's acting." Of course, Seamus's father was an actor, so he had an eye for things like that.

We walked along the road, Grivnek capering a few

yards before us. After a while he set out across a field, falling down every now and then. We continued on our way.

"Ooo! Look at the dreamboat!" Big Audrey whispered to me. There was a boy tending a garlic patch. He had thick, low-set eyebrows, pale, luminous skin, thick black hair cropped short, sensitive fat little hands, a tiny, perfect nose, and a sweet round face.

"He is cute," I whispered back.

"He's looking at us," Big Audrey whispered.

"Strangers!" the boy said. "Maidens! Swains! Travelers! You see before you the most unhappy Viknik! Life is hollow and empty! Mock me if you wish! Throw clods of earth at me! I do not care! Nothing could make me more wretched and miserable."

"Ooh, he's tragic," Big Audrey said.

I felt a strange familiarity with this kid.

"So, your name is Viknik," Seamus said.

"Yes."

"And you're depressed about something?"

"Yes."

"May we approach?"

"Yes. Don't tread on the garlic."

We introduced ourselves to Viknik and followed him to the shade of a tree. He sat on the ground and continued looking sad.

"So, what has you so bummed out?" Neddie asked Viknik.

"Everything. Life, circumstances, fate."

"But specifically?"

"My people, the whole Valley of the Shlerm, are under the yoke of oppression. The puppet Uncle, misguided and controlled by his council of helpers, who are all witches, and not the nice kind, squeezes the very life out of everyone. We are impoverished. We are not allowed to follow our ancient traditions. We are enslaved. You know about this?"

"We met Grivnek. He told us something about it."

"Grivnek! He is an idiot!" Viknik said.

"Well, yes."

"I don't suppose he told you that the entire valley is under an evil spell."

"No, he didn't actually mention that."

"Well, it is. Those helpers of Uncle's have put an enchantment on us. Every night we sit in our little houses, enchanted. It's extremely boring."

"And this is why you're sad. Perfectly understandable."

"No! That is not why I am sad! I am sad because the men of the Shlermental are shameful cowards. We could throw off the oppression of the council of helpers, but none of them has the nerve."

"You mean by violent revolution? Against witches?

We've recently had an experience with a witch, and it was a close call getting away," Seamus said. "I can see why people would hesitate to take on a whole council of them, especially if they are not the nice kind."

"It would not need a violent revolution. It would take an act of courage by as few as three—but in the whole valley there is only one willing to do it. Can you believe that?"

"That one is you, isn't it?" I asked.

"Yes, cat-whiskered maiden," Viknik said. "I would go this minute and face every danger to retrieve the sacred amulet of which our legends tell."

"There's a sacred amulet?" Neddie asked.

"There is. And if we were in possession of it, the power of the helpers would melt away. But to get it would require entering the dark forest, seeking permission from the king of the ravens who live there, and then going through the quivering bog, which no one in living memory has survived. Also, it would be necessary to get a corn muffin to give the king of the ravens, but that part is fairly simple."

"So, you get a corn muffin, go to the dark forest, find the king of the ravens, give him the corn muffin, get permission to continue, go through the quivering bog, whatever that is . . ."

"It's very bad," Viknik said.

". . . and get hold of the sacred amulet, is that all?"

"More or less. If the sacred amulet was in possession of the people, the evil witches would lose their powers."

"How do you know it would work?" Big Audrey asked.

"Do I question your beliefs?" Viknik asked.

CHAPTER 58

What?

"Tell me about this sacred amulet," Neddie said.

"It is very ancient. No one knows where it comes from. It is believed that the person who has it can defeat the forces of evil."

"This sounds oddly familiar," Seamus said. "Tell us more."

"Well, long ago, Shmoonik, a great wizard, hid it in the quivering bog. Only the ravens know where to find it. He put it there so it would be safe, and if there was ever the need, if the people of the valley were in deep trouble, some heroes could go and find it. It is believed that no one person can do this—it would take at least three. And as I have told you, I am the only one willing to try."

"What does the amulet look like?" Neddie asked.

"It is a small carved turtle," Viknik said.

"Did you say a turtle?" Neddie asked.

"A turtle." Neddie and Seamus looked at each other.

"Carved turtle made out of . . . ?"

"Stone."

"Really."

"Yes, why?"

"Prepare yourself," Neddie said. "I may have a big surprise for you."

Neddie dug in his pocket and then pulled out a closed fist. He held his fist out to Viknik, fingers up, then opened the fingers, revealing his little stone turtle and said, "Voilà!"

"Voilà?" Viknik said.

"Look at that!" Neddie said.

"At that? What is it?"

"It's the sacred turtle!" Neddie said, smiling triumphantly.

"No, it's not."

"Is too!"

"Do you mock Viknik?" Viknik said. "That is not the sacred turtle."

"I assure you, it is," Neddie said. "Big as life and twice as magical."

"Look," Viknik said. "Give a born Shlermentaler credit for knowing what the sacred turtle looks like. First of all, that is not even a turtle."

"It isn't?"

"Of course not! A turtle is fuzzy and cute, with long hind legs and long ears."

"Then what do you call this, a bunny?"

"If you knew what it was, why did you try to tell me it was a turtle?" Viknik asked.

"Well, where we come from, this is what we call a turtle, and it is sacred and very magical," Neddie mumbled, looking crestfallen.

"You are a foreigner, so I will not insult you by going on about how you don't know a turtle from a bunny," Viknik said. "But your . . . object will not be of any help. If you want to help me, come with me to the dark forest."

"Excellent idea!" Seamus said. "We will!"

"You will?" Viknik asked.

"We will?" we all asked.

"Certainly," Seamus said. "It sounds like swashbuckling fun."

His father's influence. Every now and then, Seamus feels the need to swashbuckle.

"If you're serious," Viknik said, "I happen to have a corn muffin in my leathern bag."

"Everybody here has a leathern bag," I whispered to Big Audrey.

"And foot rags," Big Audrey whispered back. "They all have foot rags. I'm going to get some."

"Are you both with me? We can start out right away," Viknik said.

"Both? Don't you mean all four of us?" I asked Viknik.

"Well, naturally the females will not be coming with us," Viknik said. "You girls can stay and guard the garlic patch, and feed the skunks."

"He's not as cute as I thought," Big Audrey whispered to me.

"Nothing doing, Garlic Boy," I said. "We all go or nobody goes. Take it or leave it."

"It's irregular. It's against our ancient traditions," Viknik said.

"Blow it out your leathern bag," I said. "That's our ancient Los Angeles tradition."

"Well, if it is your custom," Viknik said. "But I warn you, there may be scary things."

"Ha!" I said.

"Ha ha!" Big Audrey said.

CHAPTER 59

The Dark Forest

Viknik was not a good planner. If he had been, we would have waited until morning to start out for the dark forest. As it was, we arrived there a little before dark, and when it did get dark, we were already in it. There was a full moon, but only a little light made its way through the leaves. Now and then we came to a clearing, bathed in moonlight—but somehow those felt scarier than the thick trees. And we tripped on roots a lot, and stepped in holes.

"This is ridiculous," Neddie said. "We should just settle somewhere and wait for it to get light. Viknik, what have you got that's edible in your leathern bag, besides the corn muffin?"

"I have some garlic," Viknik said. "And a small fish."

"It keeps getting better and better," Big Audrey said. We all snuggled down between the roots of a big tree and tried to fall asleep.

"Maybe we can find some berries or something in the morning," Neddie said.

"Anybody want some garlic?" Viknik said. "It's first-class garlic. Besides, it keeps vampires away, and werewolves."

"There are vampires?"

"There are werewolves?"

"Sure," Viknik said. "Why do you think people are afraid to come here? See that dark shadow, sort of like a blob over there?"

We all saw it.

"Werewolf," Viknik said. The shadow moved a bit.

"Pass some of that garlic over here," Seamus said.

"I'll have some."

"Yes, me too."

"Save some for me."

Trying to sleep in the dark forest was a joke. It was like rush hour. There were werewolves—we got a good look at some of them—and vampires wandering all around, making noise. There were huge black, fire-breathing horses crashing through the forest, various nameless shrieking creatures, and the well-known things that go bump in the night. Also, we were kept awake by floating lights, strange, evil-feeling cold breezes that were like a hand stroking your face, and little skittering things, like crabs, that made a kind of horrible gibbering sound.

"It gets better in the daytime, right?" I asked Viknik.

"Never having been here before, I can't say," Viknik said. "But I imagine it does . . . somewhat."

"Who besides me is sorry he came?" I asked.

"Not me," Seamus Finn said. "This is great fun."

"Shut up, Seamus," we all said.

CHAPTER 60

Dawn in the Forest

I never thought I could fall asleep while being haunted and surrounded by noisy ghosts, monsters, and werewolves, but I found myself waking up—we all did—when the dawn filtered down through the leaves. I have to say, I felt pretty good. "I'm so hungry," I said, stretching.

Everybody else was hungry too. We found a little stream that was clean and cold, and drank, washed, and managed to get ourselves tidied up, but we didn't see anything that looked edible.

It was hard not to think about the corn muffin in Viknik's leathern bag—but, of course, we needed that to give to the king of the ravens. We were about to split Viknik's little fish five ways—it was not an appealing little fish, even to very hungry people—when we smelled something marvelous.

"What is that?" Seamus asked.

"Smells like doughnuts," Neddie said. We pushed our noses up in the air and sniffed deeply.

"Smells better than doughnuts," Big Audrey said. We were walking, almost without knowing it, in the direction of the delicious smell. In a clearing, we found a little guy of remarkable appearance frying up crullers or fritters of some sort in a big skillet, over a charcoal fire. The little guy was maybe four feet high, and it seemed like a third of that was his high-domed bald head. He had weird, large, round dark eyes that gave him a surprised or frightened expression—and there were three flashing lights in his midsection! The lights appeared to be part of him, not something he was wearing.

"You want to buy sfingi?" the little guy asked us.

"Sfingi? Those are sfingi?"

"Yes. Good. You want to buy?"

This presented a problem.

"What do you suppose they use for money around here?" I asked.

"Let's try some American coins and see if he'll accept them," Seamus said. He pulled a handful of change out of his pocket and offered it to the little guy. The little guy studied the coins, selected a nickel, sliced open five sfingi, slathered them with what turned out to be butter and honey, dusted them with powdered sugar, wrapped each in a large leaf, and handed them to us.

"Oh my goodness!" Neddie said. "I am never going to be able to go back to the Rolling Doughnut when we get home."

The rest of us said things like "Mmmph!" and "Yum!"

"This is the best thing I have ever tasted in my life," Viknik said. "And I have had the Shlermentaler fig-and-garlic pastry."

"Give him more nickels!" I said to Seamus. We ate five more sfingi. Each.

After getting to the point of not being able to think of eating another sfingi, we felt perfectly ready to continue our quest. "Let's ask the little guy where to find the king of the ravens," Seamus said.

"King of ravens? Ask giant head," the little guy told us.

"Giant head?"

The little guy jerked his thumb over his shoulder. "I guess giant head, whatever that may be, is in that direction," Big Audrey said. We left the clearing and started through the forest, going the way the little sfingi guy had pointed.

"I suppose 'giant head' refers to some local with an outsize head," I said.

"Not exactly," Seamus said. "It refers to a huge head of stupendous size."

"Why do you think that?" I asked Seamus.

"Because I can see it through the leaves. Look!"

"Holy tamales!"

It was a head as big as a house. Just a head, in the middle of a clearing. Obviously it was some kind of idol, a statue, made of stone. Only it wasn't. It was alive! "What are you looking at?" the head said, in a voice that made the ground shake.

We stood there, our mouths open.

"What? You never saw a giant head before?" the giant head asked.

Viknik got control of himself. "We need to talk to the king of the ravens," he said.

"The ravens rule this forest," the giant head said, making the ground shake. "And the king of the ravens rules the ravens. It had better be something pretty important for you to talk to the king."

CHAPTER 61

Head Games

"We seek the sacred amulet," Viknik said. "We seek the magical turtle."

"Or bunny," Neddie said under his breath.

"That's a big feat, and fairly important," the giant head said. "You kids got a corn muffin?"

"In my leathern bag," Viknik said.

"You know that to find the sacred amulet you have to cross the quivering bog, and nobody has ever done that?"

"We know that."

"And you want to see the king of the ravens, because ravens go everywhere and see everything, and you hope he will give you a hint about how to cross the bog?"

"Yes."

"All right. I'm going to let you see the king of the ravens," the giant head said. "Tell him the giant head sent you."

"Which way should we go? How do we find him?"

"Take the uptown express," the giant head said.

"The uptown express?"

"Go right through there," the giant head said, shifting its eyes. We looked in the direction the giant head was looking and saw a doorway among the trees. Over the doorway were the letters INTER-REALM TRANSIT.

"Through there?"

"What did I say?" the giant head said.

We thanked the giant head and went through the doorway. There was a flight of stairs leading down to a platform, and a train was just pulling in. We got on board. The car wasn't crowded—there were three or four ravens and a couple of trolls, reading the newspaper. We rattled along through a dark tunnel. We sat in our seats and stared at our reflections in the grimy windows and the darkness rushing past.

"How do we know when to get off?" I asked.

"I don't know," Seamus said. "It's supposed to be an express. Or we could ask a troll."

"The trolls don't look friendly."

"Or ask a raven."

"Talk to a bird?"

"Why not?"

It turned out we didn't have to ask anyone. The train pulled into a station. There was a sign on the wall: KING OF THE RAVENS. We got off the train and went upstairs. It was another clearing. On a low branch we saw the biggest raven anyone could imagine. He had on a beautiful white cape, with a stand-up collar, all covered with rubies and emeralds. He also had fancy sunglasses. There wasn't any question—this was the king.

Also in the clearing was a piano—there was a fat guy wearing a derby hat and smoking a cigar, seated at the keyboard. The fat guy was playing, and the king was listening.

"What can I do for you, babies?" the king said in a soft voice.

"The giant head said we could come see you," I said.

"Did you bring a corn muffin?"

Viknik reached into his bag and brought out the corn muffin. He handed it to the king.

"Thank ya very much. Now, tell the king your problem," the king said.

"We need to cross the quivering bog," Seamus said.

"We need to find the sacred amulet, the magic turtle," Viknik said.

"Bunny," Neddie whispered.

"Why do you want to find the magic turtle?" the king asked.

"We want to liberate the Valley of the Shlerm and get rid of Uncle and his fershlugginer helpers," Viknik said.

"Don't criticize what you don't understand, son. You never walked in that man's shoes," the king said.

"But they are oppressing us," Viknik said.

"Truth is like the sun. You can shut it out for a time, but it ain't goin' away," the king said.

"Will you tell us how to cross the quivering bog and where to find the amulet?" Neddie asked.

"What you're considering is a big feat," the king said. "Fats, sing them the song."

Fats sang a song about how somebody's feet were too big, and they looked like a fossil, and their pedal extremities were colossal. He was a great piano player, and we were all tapping our feet, big and small. At the end, we all clapped and shouted, "Yay! Yay! Your feet's too big!"

"Nice song," Big Audrey said. "Now will you tell us how to cross the quivering bog?"

"You already know," the king of the ravens said.

"Beg pardon?"

"Take the number four train to the end of the line, and start walking," the king said. "Good luck, babies, and thank ya very much . . . for the muffin."

And then he spread his enormous wings and flew off.

CHAPTER 62

Your Feat's Too Big

An hour later, we were at the edge of the quivering bog.

"Why is this called a quivering bog, anyway?" I asked.

"It just looks like some huge meadow to me."

"I know about quivering bogs," Neddie said. "We studied stuff like this in Miss Magistra's class at Brown-Sparrow. Just walk about ten feet out onto the 'meadow,' then stop and sort of bounce up and down rapidly. Then come back and I will explain it to you."

"This isn't some kind of trick, is it?" I asked Neddie.

"It's a trick, but not a dirty trick," he said. "Just do it. It will save explanation."

I walked about ten feet from where the trees stopped

growing. It felt perfectly normal, like walking on a lawn. Then I stopped and bounced up and down. The ground under my feet started to bend and bounce back, like a trampoline, and I could see ripples, like ripples on water, radiating out, maybe ten feet from where I was bouncing. I had stopped bouncing, but the bog hadn't. It was undulating and quivering under my feet. It was weird to see what looked like solid earth behaving like water, and the sensation made me feel a little sick and woozy. I walked, carefully, back to where Neddie and the other kids were standing.

"That was sort of disgusting," I said. "What's the deal?"

"Underneath, it's liquified mud and water," Neddie said. "On top is a thin layer—think of a carpet of peat and plant life, sphagnum moss, grasses. The layer is likely to be thicker close to the margins, but as you get out into the middle, it is probably thinner in places—thin enough for you to sink right through."

"And never be seen again—I get it. So, what would be wrong if we just went around, staying close to the edge, where the carpet is thicker, and crossed it that way? Why isn't that a good idea?"

"It isn't a good idea because the sacred amulet is right in the middle of the bog," Viknik said. "Ahhh!"

"Of course, there may be hummocks that are safe to walk on all the way out, and in theory we could step from one to another," Neddie said. "But how are we to know what is solid enough to support our weight, and what isn't?"

"And this is why we went to the king of the ravens," Viknik said. "All the stories say that he can tell you how to cross the quivering bog."

"Instead of which, he told us bupkis," Big Audrey said.

"Bupkis?"

"Bupkis."

"Maybe it can't be done," Neddie said. "The giant head told us that it was a big feat, and the king said the same thing. Maybe it is too big a feat."

"But he also told us we already knew how to cross the quivering bog," Seamus said.

I got it! "And we do! We know how to cross the bog!" I shouted, jumping up and down.

"We do?"

"We do! We do!" I yelled.

"We don't—anyway, I don't," Viknik said.

"We do! We were told! Remember the song?"

"The song Fats sang?"

"Yes. Your feet's too big."

"That's it!" I shouted. "Big feet for a big feat!"

"Wait a second!" Neddie said. "Are you thinking . . ."

"Yes, I am!"

"Seamus, do you have your scout knife?" Neddie asked.

"Yes."

"And I have mine. Viknik, you have some kind of knife in your bag?"

"Sure, I have a knife for cutting the garlic."

"Okay! We can do this!"

"What? What?"

"Make snowshoes," I said. "Or, in this case, bog-shoes. There are plenty of bendy saplings and reeds, and vines and creepers around here. We make big feet to distribute our weight widely, and a-bogging we shall go!"

"Oh, it's beautiful!" Seamus said. "And I have made snowshoes before, when I went to ski camp, so I know just how it's done!"

CHAPTER 63

How It's Done

It was simple. It only took about an hour. We bent flexible branches or sections of sapling into an oval and tied them fast with lengths of vine. Then we crisscrossed them with a couple of sticks, filled all the open parts with loosely woven vine or long grasses, and twisted grasses together to make loops to hold them in place on our feet. The results were crude, and wouldn't last a long time, but we were sure they would be good enough to get us across the bog.

"Let's try them out," I said.

The bog-shoes worked! It didn't take long to get used to walking on them. We discovered it was best to spread ourselves out and put our feet down gently to keep the bog from starting to quiver—but they worked! We made our way out to the middle of the quivering bog. There was a fairly large hummock, rising up a foot or so, and in the middle of that was a cairn, or pile of stones. They'd been carefully stacked, not a natural or random thing.

"I think old Shmoonik must have piled up these stones," Viknik said. He removed the top stone and reached down into a hollow that had been beneath it. He pulled out a little wooden box, covered with moss. We were all holding our breath. Viknik opened the box, and his eyes filled with tears.

"It's here," he said.

He carefully handed the box around, and each of us had a look. In the box was a little carved stone. "Oh, yes. A little stone bunny," Neddie said.

"It's a turtle," Viknik said. "I want to say that you are all great. By helping me do this feat, you have brought happiness to the people of my valley."

"What happens now?" I asked. "Do we have to do something with the amulet?"

"As I understand the legend, once the amulet is in the possession of the people, whoever is oppressing them will become powerless. I am one of the people, and I claim the turtle in the name of the people, so I would assume it will just work automatically."

"We ought to check and see if that is so," Neddie said. "Is there a way we can do that?"

"We could go to Old New Hackensack," Viknik said. "The big festival is going on there, and there will be all kinds of witches, also Uncle and his so-called helpers. We could go there and see if anything has changed."

"That's where we wanted to go in the first place," I said. "Is Old New Hackensack far from here?"

"If we continue to the other side of the bog, we will be quite close," Viknik said.

"Well, pop that amulet into your leathern bag, and let's get going," Big Audrey said.

CHAPTER 64

Supernatural Days

Looking across the quivering bog, we could see a high, skinny mountain. It didn't seem to be very far away.

"The Devil's Shoestring," Viknik said. "We head in that direction."

We headed. In less than two hours, we had arrived at Old New Hackensack. There was a big banner hanging above and across the main street of the town:

OLD NEW HACKENSACK WELCOMES YOU TO

SUPERNATURAL DAYS

The streets were alive . . . well, dead . . . with ghosts, haunts, apparitions, phantoms, and imps. Also shades, spectres, spirits, shadows, and wraiths. And there were plenty of witches, enchantresses, wizards, hexes, hags, and sorceresses. And we got to see nixies, pixies, naiads, dryads, nymphs, goblins, and fairies. There were trolls, monsters, zombies, gnomes, and leprechauns. We noticed that the ghostly types were eating! Apparently, the inability of ghosts to eat food—only sniff it—was somehow suspended during Supernatural Days, and there was no end of vendors, with stands and carts, selling everything from popcorn to roasted toads.

There were lots of beverages being offered for sale, and we saw visitors drinking from big paper cups of witches' brew. And there were souvenirs for sale: crystal balls, pointy hats, Harry Houdini lunch boxes, magic wands, T-shirts with funny slogans. We heard music coming from loudspeakers: eerie organ music, funeral dirges, and a song called "I'll Put a Spell on You" were playing so loud, we couldn't hear one another speak. There were also lots of fortunetellers, and ugly parlors, which are like beauty parlors only for witches, where you can have warts put on your nose and chin, with an extra charge for the kind with thick black hairs coming out. There were broom re-strawers, black cat groomers, and witch-shoe repairers.

We saw the ghost of Harry Houdini himself among the crowd, and Billy the Phantom Bellboy, Rin Tin Tin, Fritz the projectionist, and lots of ghosts I recognized from the

Hermione. La Brea Woman was chatting away with some other ancient ghosts, in their native language, I suppose. She smiled and waved to me. Compared to this, the ghostly Halloween parade in Los Angeles was like a tea party for babies.

"Wow! What a crowd," Big Audrey said.

"It's great!" Neddie and Seamus said.

"What do we do now?" I asked. "I mean, how are we going to tell if Viknik's having the amulet has had any effect on Uncle's bad witch helpers? The whole place is such a mob scene."

"True," Seamus said. "It's pandemonium."

"Imagine meeting you here!" someone said. It was Ken Ahara, the grad student ghost fan, looking like he was in ghostology heaven, with four cameras hanging around his neck, snapping pictures every which way. I might have known he would find his way to an event like this.

"Is this not heaven, or am I mistaken, I think not," Ken Ahara said. He looked a little unsteady on his feet.

"Have you been drinking witches' brew?" I asked him.

"I am drunk with happiness," Ken Ahara said. "Also, I haven't slept for two nights. There's just so much going on!"

"You know where everything is and when things are supposed to happen?" I asked him.

"I have the whole schedule memorized," Ken Ahara said. "Ask me anything."

"Stick with us, Ken Ahara," I said. "We will have need of you."

"Anything to oblige," the overexcited spookologist said. Then he said, "Ohhh! A zombie! I need to get a picture!"

Ken Ahara rushed off, taking pictures wildly. A hag who happened to be standing nearby, enjoying an eye-of-newt ice cream cone, said to me, "I don't suppose anyone has told that young man that pictures taken here will definitely come out blank."

"No, I don't suppose anyone has," I said.

CHAPTER 65

Perfect Opportunity

Ken Ahara came back all out of breath, from photographing, and being chased by, the zombie. It seems the zombie didn't want his picture taken.

"The big event of the whole festival is the Witch Rodeo and Ghost Olympics up on the mountain. It's tonight. There's broom flying, spell casting, teleportation, causing cow's milk to go sour, changing things into other things, and bobbing for poisoned apples. Also there is a ghostly choir and leprechaun clog dancing. Everyone is going to be there, and Uncle, who runs this whole territory, is going to make the opening speech."

It sounded pretty good. All we had to do was wait around, enjoying the sights in the town and snacking on fried dough in the shape of brooms and pointy hats, until the big show started.

"Also, this will be the perfect opportunity to see if the amulet worked," I told Viknik. "Everyone will be gathered together, including Uncle, and I assume the council of helpers will be with him. We can see if they've lost their power."

We walked up and down the streets of Old New Hackensack. The various supernatural visitors, witches, ghosts, and assorted unnatural tourists seemed happy and were having a good time. But we noticed the ordinary citizens of New Old Hackensack, and particularly the Shlermentalers, who were dressed more or less like Viknik, seemed to be slightly depressed. In spite of the festive atmosphere, I got the feeling that everyday New Old Hackensack was not a very happy place—it was the same feeling I had in New Yapyap City, though we weren't there long enough for me to be sure about it. I assumed people felt the way they did because they were ruled by a weak idiot who was controlled by evil beings.

Turning a corner, I saw a very large black rabbit, at least six feet tall, walking arm in arm with a guy in a rumpled raincoat. It was Chase! I had seen her assume different sizes, but this was the biggest yet.

"Chase!" I called out. "Where did you disappear to?"

"Ah, I see you made it," Chase said. "This is my friend Elwood. Elwood, say hello to Yggdrasil, Seamus, Neddie, and a couple of other people."

Elwood was polite and friendly. He shook hands with each of us.

"Why did you run off so fast?" I asked Chase. "We couldn't keep up with you."

"But you got here," Chase said. "Was the trip interesting?"

"Very."

"Well, that's all that matters," Chase said, smiling—if a rabbit can smile. "Look for me after the doings on the mountain are over, and I'll show you how to get home. Now Elwood and I are going to meet some people, so please excuse us." They wandered off, arm in arm.

CHAPTER 66

Witch Rodeo and Ghost Olympics

As the sun began to set, the streets began to empty. There was a long procession up the road that led out of New Old Hackensack and up the mountain. At first, I couldn't figure out how they could hold a Witch Rodeo and Ghost Olympics on a steep, skinny mountain, but then I saw there was a big open space about halfway up. It was a natural arena, with a big flat floor with gently sloping ground all around it, so everybody would have a good view. We got good seats down in front. We'd be close to the show.

"What happens first?" I asked a weird sister who was reading a program.

"First, Uncle and the council of helpers will come out and open the festivities. Next are the dancing witches," the hag said.

"This will be our chance to get a look at the council of helpers," I whispered to Viknik.

"If the amulet did its work, they should be powerless," Neddie said. "How can we tell if they're powerless?"

"I don't know. How do you look powerless?

"Maybe we should do something to get them to react," Big Audrey said. "We could try to make them mad and see what they do."

"Yes! That would work," Seamus said. "We could insult them and see if they can put a curse on us or chase us or something."

"Of course, if the amulet didn't work, we'd be in big trouble," I said.

"The amulet must have worked," Viknik said. "Our old stories, old Shmoonik—why would he have hidden it in the the quivering bog if it wasn't the real thing?"

"About old Shmoonik," Neddie asked. "Just who was he, and what is known about him?"

"He was an old wizard," Viknik said. "Very great."

"Why was he great? What made him great?"

"Well, the only story I know about him is the one about hiding the amulet," Viknik said. "That, and the various traditional names for him."

"Traditional names?"

"Yes, Old Shmoonik, Crazy Shmoonik, Shmoonik the Bungler, names like that."

"Those were his names?"

"Sure," Viknik said. "Why are you looking at me like that? He was a great wizard. One of our greatest."

"Uh-oh," Neddie said. "I hope we're not going to be bitten by wolves."

"Bitten by wolves?" I asked. "Why would you say a thing like that?"

"I don't know," Neddie said. "It just popped into my head."

"Oh, look! Here they come!"

CHAPTER 67

Which Witch?

Coming out into the middle of the big open space was someone who could only be Uncle, with a little knot of witches around him. Uncle was a tall old man. He was wearing a big ten-gallon hat that cast a shadow over his face, and a muffler wrapped around his neck and chin. Even so, I could see that he was extremely handsome. I was not prepared to like him, but for some reason I did. I liked him a lot. There was something oddly familiar about him. He walked slowly, and he looked sad.

The witches were another matter. They were cold. They were bad. They had scary eyes. Very scary. They were all smiling, which made it much worse. We could feel the crowd shrink back in fear.

"Everybody is afraid of them," I whispered to Big Audrey.

"I don't think the amulet is working," she whispered back. "They look pretty powerful to me."

"Well, I guess we'll see the show, and then look for Chase and see about starting for home," Seamus said. "Sorry about the amulet thing, Viknik, old man. It was a good try."

The council of helpers had arranged themselves behind Uncle. It looked as though he was about to speak to the crowd. Everyone was quiet. It was the silence of fear. And then, suddenly, Viknik was on his feet. "Boo! Boo! Down with the evil council! Down with fershlugginer Uncle! Free the people of the Valley of Shlerm! Boo! Boo!"

We struggled with Viknik, trying to drag him into a sitting position.

"Boo! Boo! Uncle is an idiot! Down with all bad witches!" There was no stopping him.

"Gonna get bitten by wolves," Neddie said. One of the council of helpers pushed Uncle aside and pointed at us with a long crooked finger.

"You children! Come here!"

I for one had no intention of going there. And yet I found myself on my feet and trying hard not to take a step in the direction of Uncle and the witches. The other kids were standing too, and they were also trying to resist the overwhelming urge to begin walking.

"Come here!" We all took a faltering step.

"I can't understand it," Viknik said. "Why didn't the amulet work?"

We took another step.

The witch crooked her crooked finger. "That's right. Come to us."

"Wolves, big wolves, gonna bite us all over," Neddie said.

Another step.

"Get the amulet out!" I said to Viknik. "Take it out of your bag!"

Another step.

"Wolves."

Viknik pulled the wooden box containing the amulet out of his leathern bag.

"Come to us."

Another step.

"Take it out of the box! Take it out of the box!" Viknik opened the box, removed the amulet, and held it up high.

"I hold the sacred turtle, which belongs to the people!" Viknik screamed at the top of his lungs. Instantly, I felt the weird magnetic pulling stop. The whole audience let out a sort of whooshing breath, a gasp of surprise. I looked up and saw what they were whooshing at.

It was a bubble. It was a large bubble high in the air above the middle of the stage, where Uncle and the witches were standing and looking surprised.

Inside the bubble was a pretty blond lady with a goofy smile, wearing a really silly party dress. The bubble with the lady inside was slowly descending. "Shmenda! Shmenda!" voices in the crowd said.

"What's Shmenda?" I asked the hag with the program.

"Shmenda, the good witch of the Northeast," the hag said. "Extremely good witch. So good, she's boring. But good."

CHAPTER 68

Shmenda

The bubble landed. Shmenda stepped out. Part of the audience cheered her; another part booed her. "Boo! Boo!" "Goody two-shoes!" "Sanctimonius old killjoy!" "Boo, Shmenda!" "Yaay, Shmenda!" "Yaay!" "Boo!" "Yaay!"

The helper witches were cringing and shrinking. It was obvious they were afraid of Shmenda. Uncle just stood there in his cowboy hat, looking confused. Shmenda held up her dainty little hand for silence. The crowd settled down. She turned and looked at the council of helpers, who cringed and shrank even more.

"You bad witches!" Shmenda said. "You bad, bad witches! What did you do? Shame on you! You controlled this well-intentioned but simple-minded man, and in his name you ruled the people and made everyone unhappy! And now these fine children have retrieved the magical amulet, the sacred bunny . . ."

"See?" Neddie whispered to Viknik. "I told you it was a bunny."

"It's a bunny? Then what's a turtle?" Viknik whispered back.

"I showed you," Neddie said. "Oh, never mind. Listen. Shmenda is saying more."

"Be gone!" Shmenda was saying to the council witches. "You have no power here. Now slink off!" The witches slunk off. Uncle stood where he'd been standing.

"You are not to be blamed," Shmenda said to him. "You are not evil, only weak-minded. Go and sit with the children who have accomplished this great feat. I will go now so everyone can enjoy the festivities. I know they would be eclipsed by my goodness."

"You got that right, sister!" someone in the audience yelled.

Shmenda got back into her bubble and floated away. Uncle came and sat down among us, next to me. He took off his cowboy hat and loosened his muffler. I was astonished.

The dancing witches came onstage, and everyone was clapping.

"You look exactly like my father!" I said to Uncle.

"Really?" Uncle said. "The only person I was ever told I look exactly like is my twin brother."

"You have a twin brother?"

"Identical."

"I don't suppose your name would be Herman 'Prairie Dog' Birnbaum, by any chance."

"It is!"

The dancing witches had finished and the broom jugglers were coming out. The crowd was hollering and clapping.

"I am Yggdrasil Birnbaum, your niece."

"My brother, Buck, is your father? Well, I'll be hornswoggled. Where has he been all these years?"

"Los Angeles. We're planning to go back there after the show. Why don't you come along?"

"I'd like to. It would be good to see my twin, and everyone around here knows me for a nitwit."

"They'll never notice in L.A."

CHAPTER 69

Going Home

The show just got better and better. There were spinning witches, a ghostly magic show, ectoplasmic fireworks, and the ghostly choir, which did the best singing any of us had ever heard.

"This the first time I've really been able to enjoy the show," Uncle Prairie Dog said. "Now that everyone knows I'm an idiot, and I'm not responsible for anything."

After the ghostly chariot races, and more fireworks, the entertainment came to an end and the crowd began to break up. Chase turned up. She had been looking for us.

"Let's go," she said. "The bus for Los Angeles is leaving in a few minutes."

"We're going back on a bus?" I asked.

"Sure, if you get a move on," Chase said. "Unless you feel like walking and crossing the river and all that again."

"My uncle wants to come with us," I said.

"If he wants to come, let him come," Chase said. "Just don't stand around here and make us all miss it. We'll be back in L.A. in a couple of hours."

Neddie was buying Devil's Shoestring souvenirs for his father.

"Come on, Neddie!" I called to him. "The bus will be leaving!"

Big Audrey asked if she could come with us. She said now that she had been outside New Yapyap City, she had developed a taste for travel. We invited Viknik to come too, but he wanted to stay where he was. "There's no place like Shlerm," he said.

To be continued in *The Adventures of a Cat-Whiskered Girl in Los Angeles*, now available in bookshops in Old New Hackensack, New Yapyap City, and other enlightened communities.

Take a sneak peek . . .

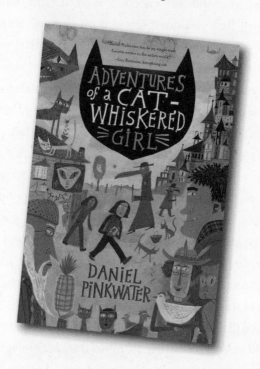

i. Explaining

It surprises me how many people don't know there are different planes of existence. Well, it's not really surprising that you don't know if no one ever explained it to you, so I will do that now. Imagine that you live in a house that is all on one level; no upstairs, no downstairs, no attic, no basement, no crawlspace underneath. You live there, and you go in and out, and everything seems normal. Now imagine that it is really a three-story house, and you live on the second floor, with people living above you and below you . . . but you never know it! You never see the people living above and below, you never hear them, you don't know anything about them—and they don't know anything about you. There are three families living in the same place, at the same time, and each family thinks they are the only one.

It's like that, only it's not houses, it's whole worlds. And there is one other thing to imagine. Imagine the three floors of the imaginary house all squashed together, so it's only one story again, but the people still have no idea they are not alone. This part is tricky to imagine. Let's say you are in your bedroom, listening to music, lying on your bed, and bouncing a rubber ball off the ceiling. At the same time, in the same space as your bedroom, someone you can't see or hear is giving the dog a bath, and someone else you can't see or hear (and the dog-bather can't see or hear) is preparing vegetable soup.

It gets more complicated. While you are bouncing a ball off the ceiling, and someone else is bathing the dog, and someone else is making soup, a highway with traffic is running right through your bedroom, or there is a herd of buffalo wandering around, or there's a river with water and fish in it. All at once, and all at the same time. But if you are in any of the worlds all going on at once, it looks and feels to you like there is only one.

Now imagine this: sometimes it is possible to go from one world to another. It's really rare, but it does happen. There you are bouncing a ball off the ceiling, and next thing you know you are in the middle of a herd of buffalo. Or, if you were to catch a momentary glimpse of someone from another plane of existence, you'd probably mistake them for a ghost. I know about all this—I myself came from another plane of existence to this one.

A skeptical person might think I was making all this up, or that I was crazy if I believed it myself. Of course, anyone can say she comes from another plane, or planet, or that her mother is the queen of Cockadoodle (which is not a real place, as far as I know). Well, it's true that I can't absolutely prove I come from another plane. However, if you go to the library and get a hold of encyclopedias and *National Geographic*s and certain books, you can find an article with pictures of a typical-looking Inuit, a typical-looking Northern European, a typical-looking Mongolian, a typical-looking Bantu, Korean, Australian, Moroccan, and so on . . . all different types. All different in minor ways, and all similar in most ways. It is interesting. What you will not find is a picture of a girl with cat whiskers and sort of catlike eyes. That is, until they take a picture of me.